THE DEFECTOR

Maggie Black Case Files #3

JACK MCSPORRAN

Series Guide

The main Maggie Black Series consists of full-length novels featuring secret agent Maggie Black.

The Maggie Black Case Files is a prequel series of self-contained missions which Maggie completed prior to the events of the main Maggie Black Series.

Both series can be read before, after, or in conjunction with the other.

Maggie Black Case Files
Book 1: Vendetta
Book 2: The Witness
Book 3: The Defector

Maggie Black Series
Book 1: Kill Order
Book 2: Hit List (Coming Spring 2018)

In loving memory of my sister, Ashley.

Chapter 1

London, Great Britain
27 December

Snow had visited the city of London.

It blanketed the streets and rooftops during the night, decorating the city like white icing on an intricate display of gingerbread. Maggie Black cupped her hands around her steaming mug of tea as snowflakes fluttered down from the heavens and swirled among passersby, each wrapped in warm scarfs and woolen hats to battle against the winter.

"Maggie?"

"Huh?" she asked, her breath clouding against the window pane.

Ashton slurped a gulp of his triple shot latte. "You were in a world of your own there."

The hum of chatter enveloped the little bookstore and coffee shop on Regent Street. People made the most of their time off to catch up with old friends. A few lone patrons sipped on cappuccinos in the corners as they clacked the keyboards of their computers, while others perused the shelves of hand-selected books curated by the owners.

Maggie pinched the bridge of her nose. "Sorry, what were you saying?"

"I missed you at the party," Ashton repeated, not quick enough to hide the glimmer of hurt behind his deep blue eyes.

"I meant to come," Maggie explained, "but I got back late from an assignment the night before and lost the entire day to jetlag."

Ashton eyed her over his mug, not buying any of it.

It wasn't a complete lie. Every spy knew the best tales were told in half-truths. Maggie *had* just returned home from a job on Christmas Eve, but it was only a two-and-a-half-hour flight away in Lisbon. Instead of heading over to Mayfair for Ashton's party, Maggie spent Christmas day curled up on her couch with a bottle of whiskey. Though she'd sat in complete darkness, she wasn't alone. Willow had stopped by to get out the rain and scrounge some turkey dinner, but the stray cat had to settle for a tin of tuna.

It was far from merry.

Maggie couldn't stomach anything else. Sitting around and pretending everything was okay required too much work, especially over the holidays. Better to slink away until the festivities were over.

Not that her best friend had any intentions of allowing her to skip seeing him.

"I got you a present," she said, changing the subject and sliding a hastily wrapped box in front of him. "It's not much. I was stuck in Portugal all of last week."

"Obrigado," Ashton said, tearing the wrapping paper off to reveal a bottle of his favorite aftershave. He took the cap off and spritzed himself with a half-dozen sprays, mortally offending a group of mothers behind him. "My favorite," he said, oblivious to them.

"I got it in duty-free," Maggie admitted, the sweet scent tickling the inside of her nose. She had pushed the holidays to the back of her mind so much she'd almost forgotten to get him anything.

Ashton hadn't forgotten her. With his spare key, he'd snuck into her apartment while she was away and delivered a bundle of presents. He'd even dug her tree out from a closet and put it up in the living room, baubles and all, and left her gifts underneath. Never one to do anything by halves, Ashton had splurged on her with designer boots and matching handbag, a twenty-year-old bottle of whiskey which she'd emptied on Christmas day, and even the latest hardback from one of her favorite writers.

"Are you going to tell me what's wrong?" Ashton asked, his playful façade gone and replaced with real concern.

Maggie balked. "What do you mean?"

"When things are bad, you hide, and you hop off on as many assignments as you can." Ashton sighed. "You haven't been yourself since you came back from New York."

"I'm fine," Maggie lied, forcing a smile before taking a prolonged sip of tea. "Work's just been busy, that's all." She didn't want to talk about New York, or what happened afterward.

Maggie's phone rumbled on the table and alerted her to an incoming call.

"Speaking of work," she said, answering before the third buzz. "Bishop."

Ashton scrunched his nose at the mention of his former boss.

"We have a situation," Bishop said, forgoing pleasantries.

Maggie sat up straight in her chair, unused to the panic that laced his words. "What is it?"

"Bomb threat. We have reason to believe it's legitimate."

"Where?" she asked, a pit of dread forming in her stomach.

"Trafalgar Square."

Maggie closed her eyes. The square would be filled

with civilians, out to enjoy the snow and gaze upon the twenty-foot tree, gifted by the Norwegians every year in thanks to the British for their help during the Second World War. "I can be there in less than ten minutes."

"Hurry," Bishop urged. "The bomb squad is on their way, but they were called out to another incident in Wembley."

"I'll call you when I get there." Maggie hung up and grabbed her coat.

"What's wrong?" Ashton asked, standing up as she fumbled with the jacket sleeves.

"We've got a situation," Maggie said, already calculating the quickest route to the square. "I have to go."

Leaving Ashton, Maggie barged out the door and took off at a run.

"Wait," Ashton yelled, following behind her. His long legs caught up to her in seconds.

"What are you doing?" Maggie quickened her pace, glad she'd chosen to wear boots for their coffee date.

Ashton steadied his pace to match hers. "I'm coming with you."

Maggie pressed her lips into a thin line. She didn't have time to argue. Together, they charged south-east down Regent Street, feet sloshing in the wet snow, grimy from a day's worth of travelers. The slush was a horrible mix of gray and brown along the edge of the pavement, shoved to the sides of the road in mounds to clear the way for traffic.

Ashton zipped his jacket up as he ran, snow dusting his jet-black hair. "Brief me."

Grit crunched under their boots as they crossed the road and continued onto Coventry Street, weaving through the crowded afternoon traffic.

"Bomb," Maggie said between puffs, her hot breaths like bursts of smoke. "Trafalgar Square."

"Fuck," Ashton hissed, picking up his pace. Maggie matched him, taking a right to remain on Coventry Street.

Bargain shoppers laden with overstuffed bags hobbled along the pavement, careful to avoid any underlying sheets of ice below the layer of snow. The soles of Maggie's sensible boots kept her steady as they sprinted through the shoppers, careful not to collide into them in an explosion of half-priced clothes and frivolous electronic goods.

Sweat trickled down Maggie's back as her body settled into the rhythmic surge of running. Counting the time in her head, she estimated a total of six minutes had passed before they reached the corner of Coventry Street and turned left into Pall Mall.

Traffic was congested, the never-ending lines of London vehicles especially thick from the added holiday tourists. The cars inched close to the backs of their neighbors, honking and waving frustrated fists at drivers who wouldn't allow them to merge in from Cockspur Street.

Maggie's heart sank as she and Ashton turned the bend and caught sight of Trafalgar Square.

Nelson's Column rose high above the crowded square,

the granite statue of the admiral looking down upon the mass of people. Majestic bronze lions languished on their stone pedestals at the column's base, and Maggie fought the urge to roar to the crowd, to warn them to run and get as far away from danger as possible.

Biting down on her lip, Maggie refrained. Alerting everyone would only worsen the situation, causing panic and mayhem as everyone tried to run to safety, pushing and shoving as the animalistic instinct to survive kicked in and ruled over all else.

"Where is it planted?" Ashton asked, hands on his knees.

Maggie ran a hand through her hair and looked around. "I don't know. Bishop never said."

Which meant he didn't know. The bomb could be anywhere.

"Let's split up." She pointed to the National Gallery with its steps and stone pillars, crowned with a dome on the roof. In the corner, St. Martin-in-the-Fields church sent a foreboding shiver down Maggie's spine. She wasn't the praying type, but they could use all the help they could get. "You take the north side. I'll take the south."

Ashton nodded, jaw set and eyes hard as he headed into the crowd and disappeared. Maggie wasted no time and rushed towards the nearest of the two fountains. Pigeons, rotund from the offerings of tourists, cawed and flapped away as Maggie stormed through their pecking grounds.

Scanning the area, Maggie searched for anything out of the ordinary. An abandoned bag. A suspicious looking man wearing a stuffed jacket to hide his suicide vest.

Nothing.

There was nothing at the other fountain, either. A well of panic rose within Maggie. Her palms grew clammy, and her head thumped as she rushed to think of where the would-be-bombers might place the device.

Somewhere that provided maximum exposure.

Somewhere that could do the most damage.

Big Ben chimed in the background, visible in the distance through Whitehall, the road that connected Trafalgar to Parliament Square. The bell rang and reverberated through the city, bellowing like the horn of war.

A sign caught Maggie's attention. A red circle with a white center. A blue stripe across the middle. The sign for Charing Cross station.

The underground.

The bell rang for the second time. Maggie turned from the fountain and made for the entrance of the station. Bishop said the bomb was in Trafalgar Square, but it could very well be *under* them.

The ground vibrated, sending thrills through Maggie's feet and up her legs. She turned back to stare at the square as her mind caught up to the sensation a split second before it happened.

Big Ben rang for the third and final time.

And chaos erupted.

A surge of energy pulsed through the square like a tidal wave and sent Maggie reeling. An earth-shattering boom thundered all around her.

Maggie landed hard on her back, the fall sucking the air from her lungs.

Debris rained over her like hailstones. A cloud of dust and crushed ruble enveloped the surroundings in a dense, opaque fog. It clung to the back of Maggie's throat as she struggled to breathe.

Ringing swarmed her muddled thoughts as pain rattled through her ruptured eardrums.

An acute stabbing sensation punctured her side, and she knew from experience that at least one of her ribs was broken.

After the echoes of the explosion faded, an eerie silence fell over the square. It couldn't have been more than a few moments, but it felt like forever as Maggie lay there on the cold, wet ground.

Then the screams came.

Guttural, primal screams laced with pure anguish.

Pushing herself into a seated position, Maggie forced her eyes open, forced herself to bear witness to the destruction she should have stopped. The horror she could have prevented. If she were quicker. Smarter. Better at her job.

The dust settled and revealed a world splattered in red, white, and gray.

Blood trickled over the upturned ground and seeped

into the snow. Bodies scattered the square, crumpled and broken. Squirming in agony, or not moving at all.

The explosion had spilled out into the road, causing a collision of vehicles down the whole right side of the square. Windows were shattered, and damaged horns blared from upturned cars.

"Mummy?" came a whimper.

Maggie followed the sound, and her eyes latched onto a small hand poking through a pile of rubble further into the heart of the square. Getting to her feet, she limped over to the mound on shaking legs and began to dig.

Chunks of uprooted ground were all over the place. Their rough surfaces scratched at Maggie's palms. She ignored the discomfort and continued removing pieces from the pile.

A woman's eye peeked through the mound, bloodshot and vacant. Maggie ignored the dead woman, led by the soft groans coming beside her body.

Shoving a heavy clump of debris to the side, Maggie gasped as the tiny frame of a boy, no older than four, came into view. He was buried from the waist down.

"Mummy?" the boy called again, barely a whisper this time.

Maggie clamped a hand over her mouth and held back the cry building behind her lips. Her eyes traveled to the dead woman and back to the woman's small son.

Moving more wreckage away from him, Maggie inched closer and wrapped her arms lightly around the little boy's upper half, the rest of him pinned under a large, unmovable cluster of rock. She couldn't move him. Couldn't risk dragging him out in case his spine was broken.

"Maggie?" An unmistakable Scottish brogue broke through the choir of confused hysteria.

"Ashton!" Maggie yelled, her bottom lip quivering at the sound of his voice.

"Mags." Ashton broke through the smog like a specter, a layer of dust coating his skin and clothes. He stumbled to her side, a red gash poking through his ripped trousers. "Are you hurt?"

"I'm fine," Maggie croaked, hoarse from coarse dust in the air. "You?"

Ashton stared down at the boy in her arms and didn't answer. He fell to his knees beside her.

"I want my mummy," mumbled the little boy, disoriented and eyelids heavy.

"Hey, hey. It's okay." Maggie blinked back tears and brushed the boy's angelic curls from his dirt-covered face. "You're going to be okay."

She shared a knowing look with Ashton, his image blurred as a track of tears ran down her grubby cheeks.

It didn't take long. Ashton sat by Maggie's side while she held the boy. He took his last, shallow breath and then was gone, his life ended before it even started.

Sirens wailed all around Trafalgar Square as Maggie bowed her head and wept.

Chapter 2

28 December

His name was Oliver Clark.

The little boy's face was one of dozens to appear on the news, including his mother, Anna. Most of the victims hadn't been identified and released to the public yet, but the death toll continued to rise as emergency services worked the scene.

Maggie leaned back against the wall of the elevator as it ascended to the fourth floor of the Unit headquarters. Bishop had called all available agents to an emergency meeting, an event so rare there hadn't been one since Maggie's recruitment.

The early call didn't bother Maggie. Since the explosion, she was lucky if she managed more than two hours of fitful sleep, little Oliver's face watching her every time she closed her eyes, his whimpers echoing through her head.

Her reflection stared back at her in the elevator's mirrored interior. Blond hair pulled back in a tight ponytail. Face make-up free and paler than usual, accompanied by dark rings under her light blue eyes. Cuts and scrapes grazed her vulpine features, reminding her how lucky she was to be alive.

The elevator cart jerked as it stopped, and Maggie hissed at the stabs of pain in her side. Some injuries were less obvious in the mirror. The doors pinged open. Maggie stepped into the hall and nearly crashed into a fellow agent.

Leon.

Maggie sucked in a breath and froze, her legs rooted to the ground. Her throat tightened, and before she could walk away and retreat into the elevator, he turned around.

"Maggie." Leon wrapped his strong arms around her in a fierce embrace. "Are you okay?"

It took every ounce of her training to keep from falling to pieces in his arms. To bury the hurt and fears instead of dumping them all over his shoulders. A part of her almost laughed at his question. She wasn't okay. Hadn't been for a while now.

The familiar, masculine scent of him mixed with his woody aftershave and the mint-infused soap he always used. Maggie inhaled it like air and tried to keep a lid on the emotions bubbling inside her.

"I've been trying to call you," he said, still holding her, longer than a colleague should. A few of the agents waiting in the lobby eyed them, but Maggie didn't care. She held on, too, resting her forehead into his chest as her body tingled with the warmth of his touch. She'd been so cold lately. Cut off from everything. Frozen in her grief.

"I know." Maggie couldn't say more without everything, all her secrets, spilling out. She'd been avoiding him since her miscarriage. She couldn't even imagine where that conversation would start. Or how.

"That message you left. You said you had something to tell me?" Leon broke his hold but stayed close, their bodies inches apart. "Something you didn't want to say over the phone?"

Warm, deep brown eyes studied her. His brow furrowed at what he saw, concern mapping Loen's beautiful, rugged face.

Leon deserved to know. Yet if she told him about her loss, about *their* loss... No. She couldn't hurt him like that. A piece of her had shattered when the doctor delivered the bad news. Maggie wasn't sure it would ever heal. She couldn't do that to Leon.

"I–" she began, scrambling for something else to say.

"All right, people," Brice Bishop called, saving Maggie from having to say more.

Everyone waiting in the floor lobby turned to their boss and chief of the Unit. "Now that we're all here let's get started."

"We'll talk later," Leon said, holding the door of Bishop's office open for her as they entered.

Maggie nodded and slipped inside, crossing to the back of the office and sitting next to her fellow agent, and one of the few other women on the team, Nina Crawford.

The aroma of bad instant coffee filled the crowded room, some of her colleagues bleary-eyed with rumpled clothes, showing signs of jet lag.

"Bishop called some of us in from the field," Nina whispered when Maggie took in her less than pristine appearance. "I'd just landed in Frankfurt and had to jump on a flight straight back. The director made it clear this took precedence over everything else."

Maggie nudged her head to the door. "Speak of the devil."

Director-General Helmsley entered the crowded room, impeccable in her black skirt suit and wearing a grim expression. A sharp bob of gray hair framed her face, and she regarded her agents with sharp eyes that missed nothing. "All right, enough chit-chat."

Agents took the seats at the large conference table, and the rest lined the back wall as the room fell quiet.

Bishop stood to the director's right-hand side and clicked on the projector. Images of the disaster in Trafalgar Square appeared on the wide screen. Maggie averted her eyes and focused on the Unit leaders. She'd seen enough in person yesterday.

The director addressed her agents. "As most of you

know by now, at exactly three p.m. yesterday, we experienced one of the worst terrorist attacks since the bombings in 2005. A self-proclaimed branch of ISIS, known as the Acolytes of the Holy War, has already claimed it as their own."

"Where are they from?" asked Zayan Asad. Of all the agents present, he had the most experience in dealing with terrorist cells. Infiltration mostly. Deep, and dangerous, undercover work.

Helmsley's lips thinned. "Unfortunately, this group is homegrown. Radicalized right here in London."

Bishop pressed the remote again, and the ruined square was replaced with blueprints. "The terrorists planted explosives in the disused Jubilee Line. It runs under the square, passing directly beneath the destroyed fountain."

"Why Trafalgar Square, specifically?" another agent asked, studying the screen.

Bishop flicked to an image of the Charing Cross entrance south of the square. "We believe they were targeting the tube station."

"Charing Cross is regarded as the notional center of London," Nina said, thumbing through copies of the images and blueprints left on the conference table. "It's the point from which distances from London are measured."

"They hit us at our core," Leon said from across the table, his voice almost a growl. "Right in the heart of our city."

Maggie leaned back in her chair and crossed her arms. "These aren't some explosion-happy, unorganized terrorists. They put thought into their target, picking a place that sends a message, not just to Britain, but the whole world. The Acolytes used the square as a symbol. These people are coming at us, but from within."

"This video certainly backs your theory, Maggie." Bishop pressed another button on his remote, and the screen switched to a loading video. "The Acolytes posted this online an hour ago."

The video played and revealed a bearded man dressed in miscellaneous military gear. The Black Flag was pinned behind him as he spoke in Arabic, a language Maggie recognized but didn't speak. A dark glint shone in his eyes, matching the smug grin slashed across his face.

Bishop paused the clip. "This is Dabir Omar. He's been on Counter Terrorism's radar for a while, but they were unable to formally tie him to anything. This is the first time he's shown his hand. He's not saying anything we haven't heard before. Disbelievers. Infidels. We're going to destroy the West. The usual rhetoric of these groups. What we're more interested in, is this man."

Fast-forwarding Dabir's vehement speech, Bishop stopped when the camera shifted to include another figure in the frame. The boy was no older than eighteen. Baby-faced, with a mop of dark hair and a dusting of fluff across his jaw, evidence of a failed attempt at growing a beard.

"Hakim Hasan," Bishop continued. "You might recognize the surname from his brother, Khalid, who was responsible for a previous attack in Belgium two years ago, killing ten civilians and himself. It appears Hakim is following in his brother's footsteps."

Director-General Helmsley caught each of their gazes and paced as she spoke. "Like many vulnerable Muslim youths, Hakim and his brother were targeted by The Acolytes online. They manipulated them, twisting their worldview with their jihadist ideologies and recruited them into their ranks. Now he's being used to recruit others."

Bishop hit play again, and they all watched the remainder of the clip.

"My name is Hakim Hasan," the boy said in a thick Birmingham accent. "This is my plea to those of you like me. To those who are sick and tired of being treated like dirt. Too long has the West viewed us as second-class citizens. They've led us down an unrighteous path, and we're suffering because of it."

Hakim was dressed in a trendy t-shirt and jeans, likely a deliberate move on Dabir's part to make him appear more relatable.

"It's not too late," Hakim continued in the recording. "You know what's right. You know we can't let them keep their foot on our necks. I was blind, like you are, too busy worrying about getting with girls and my plans for the weekend. But I see now. It's time for us to rise against our enemies. We will not stop. We will not falter. The Day of

Judgement is coming, and you owe Allah your allegiance."

Hakim reached for the camera and peered down the lens. "Au revoir."

The video ended there, and Bishop turned off the projector.

"Au revoir," Zayan mirrored. "That's rather bold."

Leon huffed. "Reckless, more like."

"Do we think this is another decoy," Maggie asked. "Like the false bomb scare in Wembley?" She was sure Dabir and his group were behind that, too, sending the bomb squad on a detour to allow them to attack unimpeded.

Director Helmsley shook her head, still pacing the room with pent-up rage. "I don't think so. If they can so boldly hint that France is their next target and still pull it off, it makes them appear more powerful. Untouchable."

"Not to mention the terror it's already instilled in the French people," Bishop added, sitting down at the head of the table. He sipped from a cup of what must be lukewarm tea by now and winced.

"Paris is the most likely location," Nina said. She and Maggie were both familiar with the city after being taught French by a zealous Parisian back in their training days.

"The French government seem to agree," Bishop said.

Leon tossed the copied documents he was reading over on the table and sighed. "What are the French doing about it?"

"They're on high alert and preparing as best they can," Bishop reported, refilling his cup with warm tea from the large teapot in the middle of the table. "Police are making their rounds through their watch lists as we speak."

"I don't care what the French are doing," Helmsley snapped, yanking her chair out and sitting down. "This group is our problem. They originated here, and *we* will be the ones to end them."

"Most of you will be placed here," Bishop said, filling the director's empty cup and sliding it in front of her. "We can't rule out the possibility of a repeat attack. Even if The Acolytes have left for France, their actions could spark a string of copycats."

Maggie agreed. It wouldn't be the first time a slew of smaller attacks happened in the aftermath of a hit. It awoke courage in their sympathizers, emboldening some of them enough to act.

Agent Sana Jafri let out a frustrated groan from across the table. "We'll also need to watch out for a rise in hate crimes. Muslims face enough Islamophobia in this country without people like Dabir adding fuel to the fire. An attack this size puts a giant bullseye on anyone who even *looks* Muslim or Middle Eastern." Sana glared at the screen, where Hakim's face stood frozen where Bishop paused the video. "If we're not careful, a lot of innocent people will be hurt, and any progress we've made toward building community will be ruined."

"You're right, Agent Jafri." Tea sloshed from the director's cup as she slammed in on the table. "As such, I want half of you working the streets and the rest with the online analysts. If they've left any virtual tracks, I want to know about them. These bastards need to be weeded out, once and for all."

Bishop mopped the spilled tea with a napkin. "The French made it clear they don't need, or even *want*, our assistance and are confident in their ability to find the terrorists before they strike. Quite frankly, we're not. Which is why one of you will go and find them first."

"Once found, you will alert the French to their location, but *we* want Hakim," Director Helmsley said. "And we want him brought in alive."

Some of the other agents stirred in their seats.

"After what he and the rest of them did?" spat Nina.

The director regarded Nina from the corner of her eye, unused to being questioned. "It's vital that we understand exactly *how* The Acolytes recruited Hakim. We can't afford for this problem to continue. Once the target has been apprehended, we'll send a team to transport him to a secure location."

They all knew what that meant. Helmsley and the higher-ups wanted their hands on Hakim, but that didn't mean the rest of the country would know about it. Like the Unit itself, their apprehension of Hakim would remain a secret. As would their methods to extract the information they required.

Sana Jafri stood from her chair. "I'll go."

Bishop shook his head. "Under any other circumstance, I would gladly send you, Agent Jafri. But not in this case."

Sana's hands curled into fists, her voice shaking in controlled rage. "Why not?"

"Whoever goes needs to be able to stay under the radar," said Zayan Asad, sharing a knowing look with Sana. "Given the high alert and resulting profiling from the French, you and I would stick out like sore thumbs."

Director-General Helmsley nodded. "Precisely. Besides, I need you both to lead the teams on the ground here."

"Very well." Sana let out a weary sigh and sat back down.

"In that case, this one's mine," Maggie said.

Everyone turned their attention to her.

"You're sure?" Helmsley asked, her boss's stare boring into her as she regarded Maggie's request.

Maggie gripped the edge of the table so hard it hurt. If anyone were going on the assignment, it would be her. "Positive."

"Stay behind then, Agent Black." Helmsley pointed to the door. "The rest of you get moving. I expect results, and fast."

Leon nodded in grim understanding to Maggie before he got up and left with the others. Some things were personal, no matter how detached you tried to be.

Maggie had a score to settle, and she would not fail. She was going to track down the Acolytes and bring in Hakim Hasan.

Chapter 3

29 December
Paris, France

Maggie arrived at Charles de Gaulle airport a little after midday. The flight from London was a quick hour and fifteen minutes over the English Channel, which didn't give Maggie much time to dive into the chunky paperback she bought before boarding.

A rental car waited for her in one of the large parking lots, a sleek yet nondescript Peugeot 208 GTi Sport in all black. It was an ideal model for some of the city's narrower streets, fast with incredible handling. Maggie tossed her suitcase in the trunk, turned the interior heating on high, and put the keys in the ignition.

With a quick check of her phone, Maggie was relieved to discover there hadn't been any new word from the Acolytes. No attacks in Paris or anywhere else in France.

Yet.

The Acolytes were in the city; Maggie could feel it in her bones. Terrorist groups of their sophistication had large networks of allies, and it was only a matter of time before they struck again. Right now, they'd be working behind the scenes, high off their success and preparing for their next hit. A hit she intended to stop.

Maggie gripped the steering wheel and focused on the road, trying to keep little Oliver at the back of her mind. The seatbelt dug into her side, and she shifted in her seat, her broken ribs complaining with every move. Digging around in her bag with her free hand, she grabbed the painkillers she'd been taking ever since the attack and gulped down two tablets.

Going out on an assignment injured, especially one as important at this, was never the best idea, but Maggie wasn't concerned. She'd been in worse states before and managed to complete the job. She didn't make a habit of failing, and she wasn't about to start now. She'd find the Acolytes and stop them even if it killed her.

The twenty-mile drive into Paris took longer than normal, the winter weather invoking an air of caution in her fellow drivers, at least by European standards. Most of the vehicles sported at least a few dents and scratches. People who complained about London traffic clearly had never driven in Paris. Maggie had found herself in many a car chase, yet even she took extra care on the Parisian streets.

Following the A3 most of the way, Maggie finally made it to Paris-Centre. Merging from the autoroute and into Quai de Bercy, she headed north-west and turned left over the Pont de Bercy. The river Seine coursed beneath her as she crossed the bridge, and Maggie stole a look at the water, releasing a deep sigh.

Despite her reasons for being there, Paris never failed to impress her with its regal beauty. As she ventured through the city, passing familiar avenues and boulevards lined with snow-dusted trees, she drank in the winter wonderland around her. Wind swirled the falling snowflakes through the air like Paris was encased in a snow globe, the light and fluffy flakes kissing Maggie's windshield before the wipers brushed them away.

The weather couldn't dampen French spirits. Cafés lined their terraces with outdoor heaters, allowing customers to enjoy the view as they cupped their warm drinks in gloved hands and snuggled into thick coats and scarves. Maggie let down the window as she passed and inhaled the aroma of rich coffee and buttery pastry that made her mouth water.

It took thirty minutes to cross the city's icy streets, but it was all worth it as she turned right from Avenue de

Suffren onto Quai Branly. The most famous sight in France had peeked out at her on the way, through gaps in apartment buildings and city parks, but seeing it up close was another thing entirely.

Standing proud and elegant, the Eiffel Tower sprouted from the ground on four legs and reached into the sky in a spear of wrought iron lattice. Snow rested over the metal, covering the outer parts of the tower in a frosted layer of white that glittered like diamonds when the sun touched it. Maggie craned her neck to take it all in, the tip just visible from inside her car.

Reluctant to tear her gaze away, Maggie focused on the road and slowed down to allow groups of excited tourists to scamper across the street. Maggie had visited the city more times than she could count, but the almost magical spark Paris stirred within her never changed.

The Pont d'lena was guarded at each end by two valiant stone warriors and their noble steeds. Maggie crossed the Seine once more over the bridge and entered Trocadero, the sixteenth of twenty neighborhoods, or *arrondissements*, that Paris was split into.

Checking the address again on her phone, Maggie traveled down Avenue de President Kennedy, a lavish residential street that lined the Seine and parked outside the building. Getting out the car, Maggie spun around and noted the Eiffel tower a mere hop, skip, and a jump away across the river. She dialed her friend's number and collected her suitcase from the trunk while it rang.

"Mags," Ashton answered, his hearty Glaswegian accent seeming out of place as she wheeled her luggage down the French street.

"You know," she said, using her shoulder to hold the phone while she punched in the passcode to enter the apartment building's lobby, "when you told me I could stay at your place, you failed to mention that it was on one of the most expensive streets in the city."

The Parisian apartment was one of Ashton's newer acquisitions, and she had yet to see it.

"Not expensive for me," Ashton chirped. "I won it in a poker game."

Maggie laughed and shook her head. "But you're terrible at poker."

Ashton was too much of a risk taker to play such a strategic game. He couldn't count cards the way he did at the blackjack tables on their first official mission as agents, and he had a habit of recklessly calling his rival players' bluffs every hand.

"Not when I cheat," Ashton said, and Maggie envisioned that mischievous smirk of his.

She waved at the concierge behind the front desk and entered the elevator to the sixth floor. "I can't win ten quid on the lottery, and you manage to finagle an entire apartment from someone."

"They were very drunk," Ashton explained.

"Clearly."

The elevator pinged, and the doors opened out into a

little hallway with a fire exit and one door. The apartment took up the entire floor, leading Maggie to estimate that Ashton's sleight of hand had won him at least a couple million euros in property.

"Right, I've got to go," Ashton said. "Talk to you soon."

Maggie said her goodbyes and slid the key into the lock. Before she could turn it, however, the knob twisted of its own accord, and the door opened from the inside.

"Bonjour madame," Ashton said, wiggling his eyebrows at her.

"Ashton?" Maggie stepped inside and closed the door behind her, lowering her voice on instinct. "What are you doing here?"

Ashton pulled her into a hug, wrapping his tattoo-covered arms tightly around her frame and planting a kiss on her forehead. "I've got some business to attend to."

Maggie eyed his sweatpants and bare feet. "Liar."

"Awright," Ashton admitted, taking Maggie's case and leading her into the main living area. "I thought I'd tag along. We've no had a wee trip away in ages."

Maggie being in Paris was hardly a 'wee trip.' Far from it. "You can't be here. If the Unit find out you're with me–"

Ashton cut her off with a wave his arm. "Relax, Mags. Those bunch of stiffs in London have enough to deal with as it is without checking to make sure their favorite agent isn't running around with a known traitor."

He shot her a wink at that last remark, but Maggie

caught the bitter tinge in the last word. Back when Ashton left the Unit, all agents were ordered not to associate with him. Maggie had made sure to keep their continued friendship a secret, especially from Bishop and Leon, who took Ashton's departure as a personal insult.

"Ashton–"

"Please," he replied, all hint of playfulness leaving his face. "I want to help. Those fuckers need to be taken down."

Maggie had never been able to blame Ashton for leaving like the others in the Unit had. Life as an agent required a certain type of personality, and though Ashton was more than qualified in intellect and skill level, his free-spirited nature didn't suit the job. It never had, even back in training.

He met her gaze with troubled, deep blue eyes. "I canny stop thinking about that wee boy."

It was easy to view Ashton as some wild playboy running around and stealing from the world's richest criminals, but Maggie knew him better than most. Back in training, he was like a little brother to her, younger than the rest and misunderstood. Deep down, he had a big heart and was always there for her when she needed him.

Maggie sighed and took off her jacket. "Okay, but we do this by the book."

Ashton saluted her. "Yes, boss."

Maggie ignored him and looked around. "Who did you

win this from, the queen?" The living room alone was the size of her entire apartment back in London.

Ashton followed her with his hands in his pockets. "Some tycoon from Dubai. From what I hear, he hadn't even stayed here once."

Like all his homes, Ashton had furnished the place with impeccable taste, no doubt with the help of some overpriced interior designer. It was minimal, making the most of the immense space, yet luxurious, with suede couches, marble flooring, and a large renaissance art piece hanging above a roaring fireplace. Overall, he'd kept it very French, which was just as well considering he had one of the best views in the city.

Maggie shook her head. If she had a place like this, she would never leave. "Idiot. He deserved to have it taken from him if he wasn't using all this."

"Agreed," Ashton said, putting an arm over her shoulders. "Want the grand tour?"

"Maybe later. Right now, I need to get out there and track down those bastards."

Maggie couldn't afford to waste any time. Not when the Acolytes were out there somewhere getting ready to deal out more devastation.

She walked over to the glass door which lead out to the full-length balcony. Boats coasted down the Seine, filled with unsuspecting tourists out exploring for the day. Beyond the Eiffel Tower, the rest of the city stretched out before her with rooftops crowned in snow. In a few hours,

the sun would set, and lights would twinkle to life, illuminating the horizon like a constellation of stars.

Amid all the beauty, a gray cloud still loomed over
Maggie's head. The city she loved wasn't safe, and neither
were the people who called it home.

"What's the plan?" Ashton asked, standing next to her.

Maggie nudged him with her elbow, trying to lighten
the situation. "Careful, Ash. You're starting to sound like
you miss your old agent days."

Ashton snorted. "Aye right. I'll crack the jokes, Mags."

"We're going to need supplies." Maggie wasn't taking
any chances on this one. If the Acolytes learned she and
Ashton were after them, the mission could turn deadly in a
heartbeat.

Ashton took her hand and led her into the master
bedroom. A row of fitted wardrobes were installed against
one wall, but there weren't just clothes inside them.
Ashton opened the center doors and revealed an arsenal fit
for a small revolution.

"Will these do?" he asked.

Maggie ran her eyes along the rows of knives, guns,
communication devices, night vision binoculars, grenades,
and if she was right, blocks of packed explosives stacked
like bricks in the corner. Ashton had better hope he never
had a fire.

"You had all this lying around?" Maggie asked.

Ashton shrugged. "You keep a fridge full of food, the

bar filled with drinks, and your secret stash of weaponry loaded and ready to go. It's called being a good host."

The packed blocks caught Maggie's eye again, and the cogs turned in her mind. There was no way the Acolytes could have transported explosives with them. Not in the volume needed to carry out another attack like Charing Cross. They'd need to restock, and the number of vendors who supplied that level of power in Paris would be a short list indeed.

Maggie turned to Ashton, who had a habit of blowing things up. "If you needed to get your hands on the kind of explosives the Acolytes use, who would you go to?"

It didn't take Ashton long to answer.

"Gabrielle Legrand."

Chapter 4

Maggie tossed the keys for her rental to the valet and took in their meeting place. Situated in Avenue Montaigne, Gabrielle Legrand's restaurant shared an exclusive address with Paris's most high-end and, in Maggie's opinion, absurdly overpriced designers. The Palais de Legrand sat nestled between Dior a few doors down at one end, and Ashton's favorite, Louis Vuitton, at the other.

"Nice, isn't it?" Ashton asked, right at home amid the extravagance. He wore a sleek dinner jacket under his tan cashmere coat, and his polished leather loafers winked up at her.

Maggie regarded the fine establishment with a raised eyebrow. "Restaurants and explosives. Bit of an odd mix in business ventures."

"Yes," Ashton said, holding the front door open for her,

"but places like these are ideal for laundering black-market money."

Stepping inside, Maggie was met with the soft melodies of a grand piano and a delicious waft from the kitchen that made her mouth water.

The maître d' was upon them immediately with a dulcet tone and warm smile. "Monsieur Price, so nice to see you. And Mademoiselle, how beautiful you look. May I take your coats?"

Maggie obliged and shrugged out of her winter coat. Ashton hadn't lied when he said Gabrielle's place was up-market. She was glad she took his advice and wore the royal blue cigarette trousers and matching tailored jacket.

Storing their coats away, the maître d' returned. "Please come with me, Madame Legrand is waiting."

He led them through the restaurant, avoiding the center floor where most of the diners sat. The décor was pristine and white, embellished with mirrored glass and crystals that sparkled in the light. The chairs were plush and high-backed, the glassware and crockery as fine and elegant as the food on the plates.

A small set of stairs brought them to a raised section with private booths that overlooked the rest of the restaurant. A woman sat alone in one of the finer booths and watched them approach. In front of her, a wide-necked man stood sentry, dressed in a well-fitted suit that did little to hide the bulging muscles of his arms and legs.

Maggie noted the surrounding tables were left empty, most likely to avoid any prying ears.

"Gabrielle, my dear," Ashton called, walking straight past the brute without so much as a nod and heading straight for their host.

"Ashton," Gabrielle replied, standing from her seat to air-kiss both of his cheeks. Her eyes never left Maggie as she did so, sizing her up with an unreadable expression. Maggie merely stared back, thanking the maître d' as he left them to their discussion.

"This is my friend, Eva," Ashton said, using one of Maggie's aliases. While not going full undercover for the meeting, they both thought it prudent to avoid using her real name.

Maggie made the first move and held out her hand to the older woman. "Bonjour."

"Hello," Gabrielle replied, accepting her hand with a smile that didn't reach her sharp gray eyes. They all sat around the booth, Ashton taking a seat right next to Gabrielle as Maggie took her place across from them.

Gabrielle Legrand was striking. In her early forties, her long raven hair fell in waves down the back of her slender frame, her high cheekbones and scarlet lips predominant features on her sculpted face. Like Maggie's alias Eva, Gabrielle could have been a model in her younger years, had she not decided to enter a far more nefarious profession.

"What happened to Henry?" Ashton enquired, nodding back to the grim looking guard.

Gabrielle let out an exaggerated sigh and placed a hand on Ashton's leg. "He disappointed me."

Maggie had the distinct impression that Henry was more than off the payroll.

"You can't find good staff these days," Ashton agreed, allowing the woman's hand to remain on his leg, even though his tastes didn't lean that way. Flirting was one of his specialties.

"You have a lovely restaurant," Maggie said in perfect French.

"You must try the house wine," Gabrielle replied. "From my own vineyard." She clicked her fingers, and a sommelier bustled up the stairs. He served each of them a glass of red and bowed before leaving.

"Superbe," Maggie said, meaning it. The wine was dry and had subtle fruity notes that tickled her taste buds on the way down. She took another sip before placing it on the table, keen to keep a clear head. They hadn't come for drinks, and Maggie was determined to learn who supplied the Acolytes.

Gabrielle leaned back and swirled her glass, the red wine like blood in her hands. "So, what brings you both to me? It's not often I have the pleasure of your company," she said to Ashton, almost accusingly.

Ashton shot her a grin and waited until her lips tugged

up before responding. "You know me, all work and no play."

Both Maggie and Gabrielle scoffed at that.

"Well, it's not a social visit this time, I'm afraid."

"A pity," Gabrielle responded, though she seemed far from surprised.

Maggie bit her tongue and allowed Ashton to start things off. It was his contact after all. "I'm in need of some information regarding a particular group of people."

Gabrielle cocked her head to the side, allowing her hair to drape over her shoulder. "And what makes you think I can help you?"

Ashton kept it casual. He leaned back in his chair and rested an arm over the back of the seat while he enjoyed the crimson wine. "These people would have been looking to shop in your particular niche of the market."

Gabrielle tutted at him, her eyes alight with interest. Whether it was over the topic of discussion or Ashton himself, Maggie couldn't quite decipher. "You know I can't discuss my clients. You wouldn't want me telling every handsome man who walked in here about the items you've acquired from me, would you?"

Ashton smirked. "Depends on how handsome."

Gabrielle let out a high-pitched laugh and leaned into him. She was very hands-on, even for a Frenchwoman, and Maggie suppressed the urge to yank her away from her friend.

"They call themselves the Acolytes of the Holy War,"

Ashton continued. "You might have seen them on the news recently?"

Gabrielle sipped her wine and quickly sobered. "Terrible business in London. Just terrible."

"I hear they're in Paris now," Maggie added, watching Gabrielle's face for any hint of recognition.

Gabrielle remained calm and relaxed as she turned her attention to Maggie, at home on her own turf. "So everyone seems to think."

"But not you?" Ashton asked, observing her too.

Gabrielle shrugged her small shoulders, bare from the strapless red dress that clung to her lithe figure. "I wouldn't know one way or the other."

"They didn't approach you?"

Their host bristled. "Come now, Ashton. People like them know there's no point in asking me for anything. Even those such as you and I must have some morals. There is a firm line I won't cross." Gabrielle flourished her point with a swipe across the air.

"Aye, you're right there." Ashton tossed back the rest of his wine, face etched in annoyance as he refilled his glass from the bottle the sommelier left. "But someone must be in bed with them."

It seemed Maggie wasn't the only one accustomed to Ashton's care-free demeanor. "I am curious," Gabrielle said, lowering her voice. "Why you of all people is interested in this group?"

"It's not good for business, having people on edge.

Everyone watching their backs. How is a man like me supposed to make a dishonest living with bloody terrorists running amok?"

Gabrielle nodded and patted his arm, keeping her jeweled hand there. "I'm sorry I couldn't be of more help to you. You'll both stay for lunch though, yes? I'll have my head chef prepare us something exquisite."

"As long as you're in the sharing mood when it comes to information on your competitors," Ashton said, the mischief back in his tone.

A sly smile twitched across Gabrielle's face, illuminating the cunning behind the woman's beauty. "If you intend to make business difficult for them, then you have my full disclosure on that front."

Ashton clinked his glass with hers. "Deal."

"Excellent." Gabrielle brightened and got up from the booth. "I'll go and have a word with the chef on the way to the little girls' room. Please excuse me."

"Well, if she didn't give the Acolytes what they need, that leaves only two more leads," Ashton said after Gabrielle left with her bodyguard in tow. "Fingers crossed she can tell us more about them."

Maggie ran a finger around the rim of her glass, staring at Gabrielle's empty seat.

"What?" Ashton asked, knowing her well enough to spot when her mind was running.

"I'll be right back." Maggie got up and took her clutch bag with her. "Nature calls."

Following Gabrielle's path, Maggie walked past the rest of the diners and through a set of doors. Signs for the bathrooms navigated Maggie past the entrance for the kitchens and down a wide set of stairs. The old building retained its original moldings which encompassed the high ceilings. The thick stone walls, covered with a golden filigree wallpaper, blocked out the noise from the floor above.

Gabrielle's guard stood outside one of three doors, indicating which one was the ladies' room. Maggie made to enter, but the big man's wide frame blocked the door. "Excuse me. I need to use the bathroom."

The brute shook his head.

"This is ridiculous," Maggie went off, speaking in rapid French as she opened her clutch. "Is this how your boss expects you to treat her guests? I expected more from a place that charges thirty euros for a bowl of soup. Just you wait until I get home. I'm leaving a scathing review of this restaurant on every website I can think of."

Maggie checked over her shoulder to make sure no one was wandering down the stairs, then snatched the Taser out her bag. She aimed it at the man's thick neck and clamped her thumb on the button.

Electricity crackled out the device and hit the bodyguard with enough volts to render him useless.

Using the momentum of his fall, Maggie shoved the convulsing man, pushing him past the men's toilet and into the third door. It swung open to reveal a closet filled with cleaning supplies and piles of spare napkins and tablecloths.

The volts continued to course through the bodyguard, and Maggie waited until a wet patch expanded across the center of his gray trousers before relenting. He slid down the wall, unconscious and, thanks to Maggie, soon to be unemployed.

Maggie popped the Taser back in her bag and returned to the hallway. With no one guarding the bathroom anymore, she slipped inside and locked the door behind her. Only one stall was occupied, and Maggie busied herself by the sink as she waited, reapplying her lipstick.

The toilet flushed, and Gabrielle came out, seeming more than a little annoyed to find Maggie there. She frowned at the door, no doubt internally cursing her bodyguard, before plastering on that fake smile of hers.

Her heels clicked on the tiled floor, and she stopped to wash her hands. "It's not like Ashton to bring along friends. Have you been seeing him long?"

Maggie smacked her lips and dropped the lipstick into her bag before snapping it closed. "I don't have time for this."

Gabrielle blinked. "Excuse me?"

"Drop the bullshit, Gabrielle," Maggie said, crossing her arms. "When did the Acolytes come to you?"

"I already told Ashton–" Legrand began.

"Yes, yes, you're a convincing liar," Maggie interrupted, stepping towards her with each word. "Unfortunately for you, I'm better, and I know you're not telling the truth."

Gabrielle stepped back until she was pressed against the wall. She made to bite back, but Maggie held up a finger.

"We can do this the easy way or the hard way. Your guard didn't seem to like the hard way, but I must admit it was nice to let off some steam."

"You're crazy," Gabrielle said, unable to mask the alarm behind her eyes. She made to leave, but Maggie blocked her path.

"I'll give you one last chance to tell me everything you know about the Acolytes before I force it out of you."

"I'm leaving, and I want you out of my restaurant. Claude!" Gabrielle barged forward, calling for her bodyguard as she tried to shove past Maggie.

Maggie caught Gabrielle's hand and gave it a vicious twist. "Claude's sleeping right now, but I promise I'll keep you awake for every painful minute."

Gabrielle groaned, but to her credit, she refrained from screaming. Her jaw clenched in anger, but Maggie saw the fear there, too, and she held her with ease.

"This could have gone a lot easier," Maggie said. She wasn't the tallest, but she had a few inches on the petite woman, and she made the most of it.

Gabrielle's lips curled with venom, and she spat in Maggie's face.

Maggie had tried to keep her cool, pushing down the rage that lingered just under the surface. Oliver Clark's face flashed in her mind. The cries of pain and horror echoed in her ears. The acrid smell of used explosives, blood, and destruction that surrounded the square in the aftermath of the explosion filled her nostrils.

She wiped the spittle off her cheek and took a deep, shaking breath.

Then she snapped.

Maggie dragged Gabrielle by the wrist, holding her in a painful lock that would send sharp stabs up her arm. Cold water poured from the faucet while Maggie jammed in the plug with her free hand and waited for the levels to rise.

"I've met some sick people in my life," Maggie said as Gabrielle squirmed in her hold, "but for the life of me, I don't understand how you can deal with monsters like them. They plan to blow up your own city for god's sake."

"Let me go," Gabrielle cried, the pain intensifying in her wrist each time she tried to pull back.

Maggie relished the panic in Gabrielle's eyes. The shuddering of her body as she stared at the filling sink.

"I was there, in the London bombing," Maggie said in Gabrielle's ear. "A toddler died in my arms. An innocent little boy who didn't deserve to suffer like that. None of them did."

Maggie grabbed the back of Gabrielle's head and dunked her under the water.

Gabrielle fought against her hold, trying to launch her head back and out of the water, but Maggie held steadfast. Water sloshed over the sink as Legrand thrashed around, glistening over the gleaming white tiles.

"Please," Gabrielle rasped when Maggie yanked her hair and pulled her head out of the water.

"You want more? Okay." Maggie forced her back under, Gabrielle's pleading nothing but gurgles and air bubbles.

People like Gabrielle were the scum of the earth, profiting from people's terror. They supplied groups like the Acolytes the tools they needed without the slightest thought or concern for the victims. As long as the price was right. As long as they were able to fill their pockets.

Maggie let Gabrielle up again, holding on longer this time. Gabrielle gasped for air, her makeup running down her face. "I don't know anything," she yelled between coughs of water that dripped down her chin. Her dressed was soaked, the red deepening to the color of all the blood that would be spilled if the Acolytes attacked again.

"Lies!" Maggie yelled, shoving her back down as the tap kept on running to replenish the sink. Water soaked into the sleeves of her jacket and ran up the arms, Gabrielle's scratching fingers sliding off the slick fabric.

The noises were horrible, but nothing compared to the whimpers of little Oliver. His unanswered calls to his mother. He was dead, and Gabrielle was in business with the people responsible. She didn't deserve mercy.

"Maggie? Are you in there?" Ashton banged his fist against the door.

Maggie snapped her head towards his voice and the locked door. Gabrielle wriggled in her arms and managed to raise her head out the sink amid the distraction.

"Help!" Gabrielle cried.

A bang clattered against the door, and it thrashed open on the second hit as Ashton kicked it in, busting the lock.

"What are you doing?" he called, running through the puddles of water to Maggie.

"She gave them the explosives," Maggie said, not letting Gabrielle go. "I know it."

"I don't know what she's talking about," Gabrielle pleaded. "Ashton, get her off me."

Maggie cut Gabrielle off and submerged her head again.

"Maggie!"

"She's in on this," she said above the splashing.

Ashton came behind Maggie and pried her fingers from Gabrielle's hair. "If she is, she's not going to be any use to us dead."

Gabrielle came back up, coughing water from her lungs. Maggie shoved her to the floor, and Legrand slid across the wet tiles, landing with a hard slap.

"I'll deal with her," Ashton warned, as Maggie stood panting.

"Keep her away from me," Gabrielle cried, whimpering from behind the mop of sodden hair that curtained her face.

Ashton walked over to Gabrielle and squatted down next to her. He tucked some of her hair behind her ear and pointed over to Maggie. "I'd start talking if I were you. My friend here seems to believe you supplied these Acolytes, and I don't know what will happen if I let her at you again."

"All right." Gabrielle's shoulders slumped in defeat, her fingers tremoring as she clutched her neck. "I did it. I gave them what they wanted."

Maggie stepped forward, balling her fists. "You piece of shit!"

Gabrielle backed away and quivered against the wall as Ashton interjected and held Maggie back.

"How much?" Maggie demanded. How much did the lives of innocent people go for these days?

"Enough." Gabrielle's voice cracked as fear-ridden tears ran mascara tracks down each side of her face.

"For what?" Maggie asked, refraining from hoisting Ashton off her and lunging for Gabrielle. "An attack like London?"

Gabrielle's bottom lip quivered. "Bigger."

Ashton, making sure Maggie stayed where she was, returned to Gabrielle and muttered about his new shoes getting wet. "When did you meet with the Acolytes?"

"Everything was done over the phone," Gabrielle

cried, the words tumbling out her mouth. "I spoke with their leader, Dabir, yesterday."

"And where are the explosives now?"

"They wanted them delivered. I sent them this morning."

Ashton brought out his phone from inside his dinner jacket. "I'm going to need an address."

Maggie filed away the address as Gabrielle filled them in, her sights already turning to Dabir and his soldiers. There was a special place in hell for the Gabrielle's of the world, but she was just a supplier. The real threat was still out there, and now they were armed.

Ashton straightened his jacket and motioned for Maggie to leave with him. They had the address. They needed to get going. Maggie collected her clutch and opened it again, stalking towards Gabrielle.

"Wait," she stammered, trying to crawl away from Maggie. "What are you doing? I told you what you wanted to know."

"Don't worry. You won't have to sit here long." Maggie took out the handcuffs and dragged Gabrielle to the nearby radiator. She swung the cuffs around the metal pipe and secured both of Gabrielle's wrists, locking her in place and making sure to fit the bracelets extra tight. "The police will come and pick you up soon."

Maggie would keep the location of the Acolytes a secret from the French until she had Hakim in custody, but that didn't mean she needed to keep them in the dark about Gabrielle. "I hope you can take better care of your-self in prison. Even the worst of criminals in there won't take too kindly to terrorist enablers."

Spinning on her heels, Maggie made for the door.

"But –"

Maggie shushed Gabrielle and glanced at her over her shoulder. "Oh, and don't give the police that address. I'd hate to have to repay you a visit."

Chapter 5

Beyond the City of Lights lay suburban areas the French refer to as *banlieues*. Many of these communities reminded Maggie of the council estates back home. Run down, underfunded, and tossed from the minds of the more fortunate like yesterday's trash.

"It's like night and day," Maggie said to Ashton as they drove through Saint-Denis, one of the more notorious banlieues on the outskirts of Paris. A mere thirty minutes away by train, it lay north of the city and was a far cry from Ashton's fancy French neighborhood.

"It's worse than Easterhouse," Ashton replied, sitting in the passenger seat of their rental car. While wealthy now, Ashton hadn't come from money, and from the stories he'd told Maggie, he grew up in a place, not unlike this one outside of Glasgow.

Their car had earned more than a few envious and suspicious glances from those they passed. Ideally, Maggie would have acquired a more fitting vehicle to blend in, but they were short on time now that the Acolytes had what they needed from Gabrielle Legrand.

Concrete towers loomed over them as they snaked through uneven roads, bleak and industrial looking. The gray apartment towers housed some of the most impoverished people in the area, a lot of them immigrants from war-torn places like Syria. Weeds grew between the cracked tarmac of the carparks below, the surrounding playparks desolate and filled with loitering drug dealers instead of happy children on swings.

Maggie had spent time in similar places during her youth. Seeking shelter in abandoned squats and in the stairwells of high-rise flats to stay off the cold, rainy streets. Occasionally, someone would take pity on her and allow her sleep on their couch, but she never overstayed her welcome. Certain people expected things in return, things she would not give them.

Maggie brushed the thoughts of her past away and focused on the present. According to the Sat-Nav installed in the car, the address Gabrielle gave them was around the corner.

"Saint-Denis," Ashton said as Maggie parked the car and killed the engine. "The name rings a bell."

"It made the news during the 2015 attacks," Maggie said. Paris was no stranger to terrorist activity, and the slew of attacks that occurred on the thirteenth of November that year were some of the worst to ever hit the city. "Abdelhamid Abaaoud was killed here in a raid after orchestrating the deaths of one-hundred-and-thirty people." Not to mention the hundreds of people injured.

"Let's hope we can find this Dabir before he pulls off something similar," Ashton said, getting out the car and collecting their supplies from the trunk.

A cold shiver ran through Maggie that had nothing to do with the winter weather. She locked the car as they left, knowing it would do little to prevent would-be thieves from taking off with it, but a stolen car was the least of their worries at the moment.

The Acolytes were shacked up in an abandoned electronics store along a row of unused shops. Battered shutters covered most of the shopfronts, French and Arabic graffiti scrawled across them and the crumbling brick walls.

Maggie and Ashton circled the building to avoid being seen, stopping at intervals to plant surveillance cameras and slipped into the building across the street from the back entrance. No one was there. The building was once a two-story house and had suffered a fire some years back from the state of it. Black, charred burn marks covered the walls, the furniture, and appliances reduced to pieces of burned wreckage and melted plastic.

They set up their watch, positioning themselves near

the window of the upstairs bedroom to give them the best view of the electronics store.

Ashton tinkered with the settings of the cameras on his computer while Maggie placed a final one on the windowsill. They were too close to risk blowing their cover by using binoculars. If spotted, the Acolytes would either evacuate or come to take them out, and Maggie couldn't be sure how many of Dabir's men lay inside. Maggie was sure of one thing though: the terrorists would be armed and unafraid to pull the trigger.

"Are we going to talk about what happened back at the restaurant?" Ashton asked, keeping his eyes on the camera feeds playing on his laptop. The other cameras they planted showed the store at different angles, front, and back. If anyone entered or left, they'd know about it.

"What's to talk about?" Maggie asked, hunkering down for what could be a long wait.

"It's not like you to lose your cool like that."

Maggie pulled her gun from her waistband and checked it over, giving her something to focus on other than Ashton, the friend who always saw too much. "Gabrielle deserved it."

"I'm not going to argue with you there, but you nearly drowned her. Not the best move when you knew she had intel we desperately needed."

Maggie sat the gun on her lap and closed her eyes. "This whole thing has me on edge."

"You've faced this kind of thing before," Ashton noted, stretching out his long legs.

"Yes, but this isn't like those other times. I've seen plenty of people die, and a lot of them by my hand at that. But Oliver–" Maggie cut herself off, hating the tremor in her voice. She gave herself a shake and allowed the uncomfortable sadness to turn into rage. Rage, she could handle. "I can't get my head around wanting to blow up innocent people. Especially from those like Hakim. He's British for god's sake."

Ashton sighed. "I don't think we'll ever understand what it's like for some of these kids. To be born British yet feeling like they don't belong. Like they're not welcome in their own country. A lot of white people don't exactly treat them like equals. Do you think kids like Hakim would turn to extremists if they weren't so ostracized?"

Maggie balked at the note of sympathy in Ashton's voice and sat up. "That doesn't mean they should join a fucking terrorist group and destroy the lives of others."

Ashton held up his hands. "Look, I'm not saying it excuses their actions, but they're not signing up to these groups because their life is fine and dandy."

"Nobody's life is perfect," Maggie countered, scrunching her face. "That's not an excuse."

"I'm not saying it is," Ashton replied, his temper rising to match her own. "But imagine growing up and seeing people like you demonized on the news every day. You're never the hero in any of the movies or TV shows you watch. You're always a villain. Just like you're the real-life villain in the eyes of half your neighbors, who equate being Muslim to being a terrorist. And it's not just the media. Politician's sprout that shite, too, knowing it'll get them votes."

"Ashton—"

"Look at Brexit! Look at all those hate-fueled debates over immigration. And don't even get me started on the rise in hate crimes. Britain is rife with Islamophobia, and until we address that, it'll only add to this problem."

Maggie made to retaliate but found she couldn't. It wasn't often Ashton got heated over something, but his cheeks had flushed red and his brows furrowed. She leaned back against the wall and considered his points. "I've never really thought of it like that." In truth, she'd never really thought much about it at all.

"Imagine how alienated these kids must feel, how hopeless to change their fate when everyone already thinks they're a terrorist anyway. Society pushes them down so hard they believe their best option is to join people like Dabir," Ashton continued. "These groups know how alone these kids feel. They know how lost, and vulnerable, and angry they are, and they take advantage of that to radicalize them."

Maggie's initial reaction was to disregard what her friend was saying. To fight against any attempt at humanizing the same people who murdered Oliver and the other innocents at Trafalgar Square. Yet his words mirrored

Director-General Helmsley's. When the director said the Acolytes were homegrown, maybe this is what she meant. That Britain had broken them down and left them vulnerable to Dabir's manipulations.

Helmsley's reasons for wanting Hakim brought in alive shifted in Maggie's mind. Became something more than simple revenge or interrogation. "The director wants to learn to understand defectors like Hakim."

"It's not that difficult," Ashton said, calmer now. "The same thing happened to you and me. Bishop recruited us just like Dabir did to Hakim and his brother. He made us feel wanted. He made us feel like we *belonged* to something greater than ourselves."

Thinking back on it, Maggie wasn't given much of a choice when it came to her recruitment. Facing a murder charge at the time, it was either go to prison or join the Unit. The decision was simple. Bishop would have known that, too.

"Yes," Maggie admitted, a wave of unease coming over her, "but we were recruited for something good, not evil. We're on the right side."

"And they believe they're on the right side," Ashton said. "From their point of view, we're the bad guys in all this. We're the reason there's so much violence against Muslims in the U.K. We're the reason they don't fit in anywhere else."

Maggie pinched her nose. "The whole thing is a mess."

"Aye," Ashton said with a sigh, pulling a flask out from his jacket. "No wonder I like a drink."

They sat in silence for a while after that, watching the screens. Maggie's head ached, and the bitter cold seeped through her jacket down to her bones. An hour passed with no activity from the electronics store, and she worried that the Acolytes had already left for their next attack. It was too early for that, though. They'd only gotten the explosives that morning.

"It's not just Oliver and the attack," Ashton said after a while. He shifted on the floor to meet her eyes. "You were like this before then."

"Like what?" Maggie scoffed.

"On edge and irritable," Ashton said, clouds puffing in the air as he spoke. "Something else is bothering you. What is it?"

"It's nothing." A muscle twitched in Maggie's jaw as she clamped her mouth shut and shook her head, afraid it might all spill out.

"Maggie..."

Maggie's heart leapt in her chest. "It's Hakim." She scrambled to her feet and grabbed her gun, pins, and needles shooting up her legs from sitting so long.

Ashton frowned, watching her fumble. "What?"

Maggie pointed to the man on the camera feed. "There. He's going out the back."

____

Chapter 6

____

Maggie hurried after Hakim on foot while Ashton raced for the car. She circled around the long way to avoid being seen by anyone else in the Acolyte's temporary camp. Hakim was the target in this chase, and Maggie wasn't about to have the tables turned on her if Hakim's comrades caught her tracking him.

Her pulse quickened. Her legs itched to stride faster, to run, but that would only draw unwanted attention. At least she and Ashton had come prepared. Maggie dug into her jacket pocket for her earpiece and slipped it into her ear.

"I've got eyes on the target," she murmured, crossing the road as Hakim turned right and headed down a side street. At least he wasn't jumping into a car. Tailing someone in a vehicle could easily result in losing them to traffic, especially in Paris. "He's heading south-west."

"Roger that," Ashton replied, the sound of a car door closing in the background. "I'll be right behind you."

From a distance, Hakim looked much the same as he did in the video. He wore jeans and a puffer jacket, his long strides indicating he was in a hurry to get to wherever he was going.

Maggie held back as much as she dared. His superiors must have warned Hakim to watch his back. He checked over his shoulder more than once in the few minutes she tailed him.

Police presence was scarce in Saint-Denis compared to the city, but they had a reputation for being heavy-handed and unfair when they did turn up. The last time Maggie was in Paris on a mission, a story made the headlines of a young man in the area being raped by the police during a violent arrest.

Then there were the residents themselves. Crime was no stranger here, and it wasn't uncommon to be mugged or threatened, even at this time of day.

Hakim walked for a mile or so before reaching a small supermarket. Maggie headed for a shopping cart to blend in as Hakim gave a final check before ducking inside.

Maggie spotted Ashton down the street in her rental, parked behind a delivery truck to stay out the way. "I'm going in."

"Be careful."

Fluorescent lights hummed above her as Maggie wheeled the cart through the store, stopping to look at the labels of random items she picked up before tossing them in. Hakim made his way towards a refrigerated unit and filled a basket with a dozen premade sandwiches and bottles of water, no doubt for his fellow Acolytes hauled up inside the abandoned store. Not that they'd ever eat them. Hakim wasn't making it back to the electronics store. Not on her watch.

"What's happening?" Ashton asked in her ear.

"He's shopping," Maggie replied, barely moving her lips as she bagged some apples. "I'm going to make an approach."

Waiting for the right moment was key to initiating contact. While usually best to allow the target to approach you, it wasn't always possible. Given the beads of sweat across Hakim's forehead and the edge in his demeanor, he was hardly in any mood to spark up conversation with a stranger.

He was a lanky guy, looking younger than his years. He was still very much a child in the face and in the awkward way he carried himself like he hadn't gotten used to a sudden growth spurt.

Maggie bided her time and gripped the handle of her shopping cart. She may not get a second chance if she botched her first approach. Hakim already appeared spooked.

When his basket was full, Hakim headed for the

check-out counter up front. As he spun, Maggie came up behind him and crashed straight into his chest in a mock collision. The bag slipped through her fingers and apples rolled out of it and across the sticky floor.

"Sorry," he stammered, bending down to catch some of the runaway fruit. "I mean, um, pardon."

"It's okay," Maggie replied in heavy accented English, her smile genuine.

Hakim hadn't even felt the prick of her needle in all the confusion. It was quick, and the needle was barely the length of a tack, but it struck true as she noted the tiny bead of blood on the back of his hand.

Apologizing again, Hakim handed over the last apple and left for the check-out counter with his back to Maggie.

"I got him," she said to Ashton, leaving her trolley in the middle of the aisle. "Meet me out front."

It wasn't over yet, and the next part wasn't as easy as a pin prick. Hakim wobbled on his feet as the clerk rang up his items. He wiped his brows and blinked a few times, the sedative kicking in full speed ahead.

Maggie was thankful there wasn't a line at the counter. Otherwise, Hakim may not have lasted. If he fainted in the store, she'd fail. She still might.

Wiping her clammy palms on her trousers, Maggie headed for the exit as Hakim pocketed his change and grabbed his stuffed shopping bag. The snow ensured the streets weren't busy, which was a small gift in what was an overall shitty week. No one was near the supermarket, and she loitered by the sliding doors as Ashton pulled the car around front.

An unsteady Hakim stumbled out the store, his feet dragging as he struggled to put one foot in front of the other. Maggie came up behind him and wrapped his arm around her shoulders in aid. Hakim was too far gone to protest, and only his confused face showed any signs that he registered something was up. He tried to speak, but his words came out slurred.

Ashton opened the trunk while still in the driver's seat, keeping the engine running. "Taxi for two," he said in her ear.

Maggie lead Hakim to the back of the car and helped him pack his bag away, double checking over her own shoulder to make sure no witnesses were around.

Certain the coast was clear, she forced Hakim into the trunk in a tangle of limbs and slammed it shut as his eyes rolled to the back of his head.

Maggie smirked, ignoring the aches from her broken ribs, and got into the passenger seat.

Hakim was hers now, and whatever plans Dabir had for his little protégé were about to go up in smoke.

They took Hakim to a lock up a couple of miles from the electronics store. Maggie closed the door and kicked away the busted lock. From the rust covering it and the screech the door made upon opening, no one had used the small garage in a long time.

It was pitch black inside the small confines. Ashton turned on the light, and the single lightbulb blinked on with a buzz, swinging above the chair where they'd secured Hakim.

Though protocol dictated that Maggie needed to call in the successful apprehension of her target, she needed to make sure there was no imminent threat of an attack first. And if there was, she needed to gather all she could from her captive.

Maggie opened one of the bottles of water Hakim had purchased and took a long drink. Then she tipped what was left over Hakim's head.

Hakim's eyes blinked open, sluggish and delayed, and the water trapped in his thick eyelashes dripped down his cheeks like tears.

"Wake up," Maggie ordered, the sharpness in her tone winning her a cautious glance from Ashton, who was likely worried about a repeat performance of the restaurant's bathroom.

Hakim groaned and winced at the harshness of the bare bulb. He tried stretching his long legs only to find them trapped within tight binds of rope. His eyes opened fully then, the effects of the injected drugs unable to contain the wild panic that coursed through him like electricity. Maggie saw it in the tightening of his muscles, and in the hollowed expression etched across his features.

His breathing grew frantic, chest heaving as he took in the little room. The bare bricks were covered in cobwebs. Cardboard boxes with long-forgotten belongings were stacked to one side, Ashton watching from the sidelines at the other.

"Nice of you to finally join us," Maggie said, securing his full attention. She crossed her arms and stepped closer, forcing him to crane his neck to meet her eyes.

"You're British," Hakim said, though not seeming particularly surprised at the fact.

Maggie sighed in exasperation, the disturbed layers of dust irritating her nostrils. "Well spotted."

"Are you Counter Terrorism?" he asked. There wasn't the scorn Maggie expected to find in his voice, though Hakim seemed far from happy to be there. His jaw clenched, and his knuckles were bone white against his brown skin.

Maggie leaned down and came level with his face. "I'm your worst fucking nightmare if you don't cooperate and answer all of my questions."

Hakim kept his mouth shut, wide eyes darting from side to side like his brain was on overdrive. Weighing his options. It wouldn't take long to choose one since there were so few available. He was trapped, and either he would talk or he wouldn't. And if he decided to keep his mouth shut? Well, Maggie had more than a few ways to loosen his tongue if it meant saving lives.

"Where is Dabir Omar?" she demanded.

Hakim raised his chin. "I don't know."

Maggie swung and smacked a backhand across Hakim's face. "This will go a lot faster, and a lot less painful for you, if you don't lie to me. So I'll ask again, where is Dabir Omar? Is he inside the electronics store?"

Hakim spat out a mouthful of blood on the floor. "He left this morning, but he doesn't tell me where he's going."

"Is he planning another attack?" Ashton asked, leaning against the wall, his face free from that mischievous grin of his. He could look more than a little intimidating when he wanted.

"Yes," Hakim said, keeping his attention on Maggie. They'd removed his puffy jacket while tying him up, and his teeth chattered as he spoke, whether, from the cold and his soaking shirt or fear, Maggie didn't know. Or care.

"Where and when?" she asked, keeping her alarm under the surface. She couldn't show any signs of weakness in front of her captive. "Is he setting it off right now?"

"No," Hakim replied. "We'd all be with him if he were, but most of us aren't told much until closer to an attack."

"Why wouldn't he tell you if you're part of his group?" Ashton asked, he and Maggie settling into a flow. They'd done this more than once in their many years of friendship.

"He tells those closest to him. Those he trusts. The ones who have been with him longer than I have." Hakim nodded to the bag of bottled water and sandwiches. "I'm a new recruit. He sends me on errands most of the time."

Maggie unzipped her jacket and swept a hand into her trouser pocket, making sure her gun peaked out at Hakim. "What do you know?"

"The next attack will be soon, and it's going to be bigger than London. Much bigger."

Ashton frowned. He kicked off the wall and came to stand by Maggie's side. "You're a bit too chatty for a terrorist. In my experience, people like you need a little persuasion before you betray your Brothers."

"I am not a *terrorist*." Hakim's voice was guttural, almost a growl.

"Of course not," Maggie said, her words dripping with sarcasm. "You joined the Acolytes of the Holy War to make new friends and fill up some free time."

"I joined to get closer to him," Hakim retorted, his breathing deep and angry now as opposed to the panicked panting before.

"Your brother, you mean?" Ashton asked.

Maggie startled. Had he really joined the Acolytes for something as sentimental as that? To somehow feel closer to his dead brother by following in his footsteps?

"No," Hakim spat. "Dabir."

"Why?" Maggie narrowed her eyes, her suspicion still on high alert. "Did he tell you he liked you? Did he listen to your problems and welcome you into his gang with open arms?"

Hakim's temper rose with each question, and Maggie continued, pushing him closer and closer to the edge. She raised her voice, almost shouting now, and shook him by the shoulders.

"He filled your head with bullshit, and you ate it up because he made you feel like you were a part of something. Didn't you?"

"You don't get it!" Hakim screamed, finally reaching his breaking point. "I joined to destroy Dabir Omar," he yelled, the vein on his neck throbbing. "From the inside."

A track of tears slipped down his face. Maggie had imagined a lot of motives for Hakim, but that was never one of them. At least now she could use his anger to get the answers she desperately needed. "Oh, I get it. You're on a one-man crusade to take out a highly connected, fanatical extremist organization by fetching them sandwiches."

"Shut up," Hakim spat, freely crying now.

"You're not even doing that right," Maggie said, stomping on one of the sandwich boxes. The plastic wrapping popped and the filling oozed out between the bread like spilled guts.

"I know more about Dabir and how he works than *you* do." Hakim pulled at his bindings, but they held fast. "If you and the rest of Counter Terrorism had done your jobs, I wouldn't have needed to do any of this."

"Why would you want to take Dabir down?" Ashton asked, his voice not harsh like Maggie's, yet not showing any hint of remorse either.

"Khalid died because of him," Hakim said, his voice breaking at the mention of his older brother. A drip of saliva hung from his lip, and despite everything, a hint of empathy rose within Maggie. Not that she could allow it to show. They had him talking now.

"Your brother died because he chose to blow himself up to kill ten innocent civilians in Belgium," Maggie pointed out, crossing her arms.

"On the orders of Dabir. He brainwashed my brother, just like he tried to brainwash me." Hakim sniffed and tried to steady himself, his eyes red and wet with tears.

Maggie noted how tired Hakim looked. His face was drawn like he hadn't eaten much in a while. Dark circles hung under his eyes, and he had an air of mental instability about him. No wonder he broke so easily. The eighteen-year-old, more a teenager than a man, was exhausted and living among people he considered his enemy.

If what he said was true.

"Khalid was a good guy before he met Dabir," Hakim continued, shaking his head like he still couldn't believe what had happened to his brother. "He was studying to become a doctor. He was going to make something of himself before he let Dabir poison his mind. It's just my mum and me now, and she's never gotten over his death. I'm going to make Dabir pay."

Maggie couldn't decide if Hakim was more brave or stupid. He was a good dose of both, either way. "Not from here you're not," she said, playing her role. "You'll be back in Britain by tonight."

"You have to let me go. I've worked too hard to get close to Dabir. I can help you get to him before anyone else gets hurt." Hakim fought against his restraints, so hard the chair almost reeled back.

Maggie caught the seat of the chair with her foot before Hakim toppled back to the floor. The legs clicked on the concrete floor, the sound echoing off the bare walls. "Prove it," she said. "Prove you're not lying about all of it."

Hakim looked up at her, his face defeated and pleading. "I can't."

"Then you can't possibly expect me to believe a word you say," Maggie said. As convincing as he was, the risk was too high to go on his word alone. She had orders to hand him over to the director, and she would need a very good reason to defy that command.

"The video," Hakim said with a desperate look of hope. "Did you see the video?"

"I did," Maggie said, recalling his vitriol towards the West. "You gave quite the speech."

Hakim blanched at that, knowing how he must have sounded and how it hardly helped him plead his case now. "Then you heard my clue at the end. Au revoir. Is that how you found me here?"

Maggie didn't respond, sharing a masked look with

Ashton. Had what she and the rest of the Unit considered a pompous, arrogant move on the Acolytes' part actually been Hakim's plot to give away their next target?

"I tried to warn you about Trafalgar Square, too," he continued, eager now. "I called in and reported the bomb, but I don't think they took me seriously. Dabir had already called one in at Wembley to lure the bomb squad away from the area. You have to believe me. I didn't want any of it to happen."

Bishop had said they received word of a bomb scare when he called her that day. Maggie had never asked where too consumed with reaching the square before anything happened. After the fact, she'd forgotten about that small detail, more concerned with bigger picture.

"It'll happen again if you don't do something. I can stop this if you let me go."

Maggie stared at Hakim for a long time. Her gut said he was telling the truth, but she couldn't rely on that alone. Not with stakes as big as they were.

"I trust him," Ashton said, finally breaking the silence.

Maggie shot Ashton a glare. So much for a unified front.

"I can't let him go on mere trust," she shot back, worrying at her thumbnail. Dabir was still out there. Even if Hakim was lying about infiltrating the Acolytes to avenge his brother, he still didn't know where Dabir was. That at least, she believed. There was no way someone like Dabir would allow Hakim into their inner circle in such a short period of time. Hakim would need to prove himself before he'd be privy to such intimate details.

But could he truly help? While he may not be in-the-know about everything, Hakim had gotten close to Dabir. The men had sat side-by-side in the video the Acolytes put online. Dabir was using Hakim to lure other impressionable kids to his cause.

"What's the worst that can happen if he is lying?" Ashton said with a shrug. "He tells Dabir that Counter Terrorism is after him? He already knows that."

Ashton wasn't wrong there. Hakim still believed they were with Counter-Terrorism, and Maggie wasn't inclined to correct him. Dabir had been a threat long enough to know the British Government would chase him down after the attack in London. She had Hakim in her custody as ordered, but right now, Dabir was the one capable of dealing the most damage.

Maggie turned to Ashton. "We can keep Hakim here and go back to the electronics store. If Dabir isn't planning to attack today, we wait there until he returns and ambush him."

"He doesn't stay with us there," Hakim interrupted. "He stays away from our location as much as possible in case we're found out and raided. Dabir doesn't like to get his hands dirty. He uses people like my brother for the messy work."

Bishop had said as much during their briefing. Dabir was on Counter Terrorism's radar before Trafalgar Square, but he was smart, never incriminating himself in anything and pulling the puppet strings from afar.

"But you said he was there earlier," Maggie accused Hakim. "That he left this morning."

Hakim nodded. "Yes, he arrived to inspect a delivery of explosives. There's a lot of it."

Maggie dug her nails into her palm. She should have drowned Gabrielle Legrand after all.

"Where are the explosives now?" Ashton asked. "Are they still back at the electronics store?"

"Dabir took it all with him," Hakim said. "He didn't trust the supplier and wanted to move it as soon as possible. I helped pack the van he left in with his lieutenants."

"Shit," Maggie hissed, pacing the room now.

"If you're going to let me go, then you better do it quick," Hakim said with growing impatience. "They'll notice if I don't get back soon."

He had a point. The supermarket wasn't far from the electronics store, and by all accounts, he should have been back by now. While he may not be the most important member in the group, someone would eventually note his absence, especially if Hakim was in charge of bringing the rest of them food and water.

"We can have him wear a wire." Maggie hated being backed into a corner like this. She was out of options, and she didn't like any of the ones that remained open to her.

"Dabir's not an idiot." Hakim sighed. "Everyone entering the building is frisked and searched."

Maggie swore again and refrained from hitting something. That ruled out a tracker, too, which was a pity. A tracker had come in handy on her recent assignment in New York. Without a tracker or wire, they wouldn't be able to keep track of Hakim's whereabouts or watch his discussions for signs of betrayal or hints on where the attack would go down.

Leaps of faith didn't come easy to Maggie. Yet her current predicament didn't leave her much choice.

"Fine," Maggie said, moving to untie Hakim before she changed her mind. She whispered in his ear, steady and crystal clear. "But I promise, if you fuck me over, I won't stop until I find you. I will hunt you down and kill you, and it won't be a quick death."

"I'm not lying," Hakim assured, rubbing his wrists once they were free.

"That's good," Maggie replied, "for your sake." She looked between Hakim and Ashton, the three of them the only thing standing in the way of Dabir and his next attack. "Now, let's come up with a plan."

Chapter 7

30 December

M aggie was at her wits end. After a sleepless night of no news, her nerves were rattled, and she had picked her fingernails down to the quick.

"Why hasn't he gotten in touch with us?" she asked for the hundredth time, pacing along the length of Ashton's living room. The city stretched out before them through the balcony's glass-paned doors, quiet and untouched in its blanket of snow. For now.

Dabir could be out there, preparing for his attack, and they would be none the wiser. Hakim should have discovered *something* by now. Maggie's stomach lurched at the thought of being wrong about him. Had he played them for fools?

"He'll contact us when he has news," Ashton assured her, lounging on the couch with his feet up, sipping an espresso. "Until then, sit down and have some breakfast."

Maggie sat at the dinner table and reached for the set of knives she'd been sharpening instead of the breakfast spread of pastries and good coffee Ashton had laid out. "What if something's happened to him?" she worried, tapping a finger on the tip of one of the blades. "What if they know he's working with us?"

"How could they come to that conclusion?" Ashton licked a drop of espresso from his lower lip. "They don't even know we're here, or who we are for that matter. Hakim will reach out once he's gotten something we can use."

Ashton had left Hakim with his phone to contact them. While Hakim couldn't risk trying to smuggle it into the electronics store, he hid it nearby so he could slip outside for a few moments and text them.

But a text hadn't come through.

Perhaps no news was good news. Dabir could have canceled his plans, whatever they were. Or something could have delayed his schedule. Not that the thought did much to calm Maggie's nerves.

Her phone buzzed and rattled against the wooden table, and she and Ashton jumped. Maggie grabbed the phone and read the message on the screen.

Notre-Dame. 40 mins. It's happening today.

The phone trembled in Maggie's hands, flashes of the destruction in Trafalgar Square flooding her mind. It couldn't happen again. She couldn't allow it.

Maggie did the math, going over the quickest route to the cathedral. They could make it in time if they left immediately. Maggie gathered the knives spread out on the table, securing them to the inside of her jacket and strapping them around her ankles. She checked to make sure her gun was secured in its holster by her hip.

Ashton shoved his feet into his boots and flung on his jacket, both of them in all black with tactical clothes designed for ease of movement. They didn't talk as they rushed from the apartment and out into the cold streets. They knew what was at stake.

Traveling by car would take too long to reach their destination. On foot, even longer. Instead, Maggie and Ashton sprinted to the Gare D'Avenue du President Kennedy and descended into the Métro.

Maggie checked her phone for more messages as they caught the C train and whizzed underneath the city. No more came.

Four stops and thirteen agonizing minutes later, they arrived at the Saint-Michel – Notre-Dame station. Forgoing all niceties, Maggie and Ashton shoved their way through the crowds and emerged above ground, charging across the Petit Pont bridge to the Ile de la Cité, one of the two natural islands in the river Seine, where the cathedral lay.

Maggie's heart sank as they approached the west façade. Hundreds of tourists were outside the gothic building, braving the weather to get a glimpse of the magnificent medieval architecture of the Notre-Dame de Paris. *Our Lady of Paris.* Gargoyles and chimeras glared down at them from their perches by the bell towers, birds scattering off into the air on frantic wings as if they knew what was to come.

"Ashton..." Her voice caught in her throat. There were so many people. So many innocent lives. And there'd be just as many, if not more, inside.

"I know," said her friend, taking her hand in his. "Come on."

They entered through the far right of the three front doors, known as the Portal of Saint Anne, and broke through huddles of gaping visitors with tour guides in hand.

A table lay beyond the door, filled with candles available for purchase to burn in memory of lost loved ones. The flicker of flames twinkled star-like throughout the expansive ground floor. Maggie grimaced at them. If Hakim was right about the level of explosives Gabrielle Legrand had sold Dabir, then an inferno of naked flames was not a good idea.

The sun shone through stained glass, purple hues from the three rose windows blessing everything it touched with a warm glow. The beauty felt out of place to Maggie amid the impending danger, the depiction of Jesus hanging on the cross by the high altar more fitting to the situation.

"Where would they have planted the bomb?" Ashton asked.

Maggie moved to a framed map of their location and scanned it. There was the crypt, of course. Dabir could be mirroring Trafalgar Square by placing the explosives underground. The main floor itself had plenty of nooks and crannies, not to mention the highest density of people if maximum casualty was the goal.

"I don't know," Maggie said, the time ticking down in her head. They had less than ten minutes now, the commute taking longer than expected thanks to the weather and slippery pavements.

The bomb could be anywhere, and if they didn't find it soon, they'd all be dead.

Sweat trickled down Maggie's back. She shivered despite the stuffy warmth of her jacket. She gazed out over the crowd and watched for anything out of the ordinary. Anything that could help her narrow their search. A whole minute passed before she saw anything.

Two men, one white and the other middle eastern, slunk out of a door and hurried toward the exit. Everyone else around them peered toward the heavens, their necks arched toward the windows and ceiling, or examining the placards explaining the various artifacts that circled around the rows of pews. True tourists spoke in hushed tones or took in the history in respectful silence.

But these men were most definitely *not* tourists. The white man made eye contact with Maggie from across the pews and startled, pulling his friend into a run, shoving people out of their path.

"The north tower," Maggie said, pointing the way for Ashton. There was no time to chase after the terrorists. Grabbing her gun, Maggie sent three shots into the air as they crossed the floor.

The bangs reverberated through the cathedral, amplified by the acoustics, and sent everyone into a panic. Pandemonium erupted. People screamed and stampeded towards the nearest exit. It wasn't the best method of evacuation, but it was all Maggie could do given the circumstances, and she could only hope everyone made it out in time.

She and Ashton backtracked along the terrorists' path and barged through the door to the north tower. A man in caretaker overalls lay splayed near the foot of the stairs, his throat slashed like a garish, grinning mouth. They stepped over him and took the stone steps two at a time.

Unlike its neighbor, the north tower wasn't open to the public, making it the perfect place to go unnoticed. The muscles in Maggie's legs burned as she traveled up and up and up, passing the Virgin's Balcony and then the Colonnade. Almost four hundred steps later, they finally reached the tower.

Maggie wiped her brow as she caught her breath, searching for the explosives. "There!"

A large trunk-sized box sat in the corner by the balcony.

Maggie ran to the box and dropped to her knees. Wind whipped her hair back from her face and bit at her skin, the chill much colder this high up.

"Wait," Ashton warned, blocking her hand from opening the lid. "What if opening it triggers the fuse?"

Maggie squeezed Ashton's hand. "It's going to blow anyway."

Ashton gave her a stiff nod and kneeled beside her.

"There might still be time to get out," she said to Ashton. It wasn't exactly true if the countdown in her head was accurate, but there was no way of surviving the blow sitting this close. If he made it to the bottom of the tower, he might get out alive.

"Enough of the heroic shite, Mags. We're in this together."

Maggie didn't argue. There wasn't time. She tried to say something heartfelt but found the words trapped in her throat. She wiped her eyes and focused on the box.

Her heartbeat drummed in her ears, and she held her breath as she pried open the lid.

Both she and Ashton gasped.

It wasn't a bomb.

Maggie picked up the single piece of paper inside the otherwise empty box and read the scrawled note.

You're too late. -Dabir

"Too late?" Ashton said, reading over her shoulder. "What does he mean 'too late?'"

The answer came three seconds later when a cataclysmic boom resounded over Paris.

Chapter 8

Maggie snapped her head towards the eruption.

A surging wave of heat pulsed through the air, slamming her and Ashton back against the wall of the north tower.

Below them, water flew into the air from the Seine, blasting over the sides of the riverbanks onto the pavements and surrounding roads.

Chunks of metal and shredded bits of wood followed the flood waters, obliterated pieces of the boat that moments ago carried passengers along the Seine. The shrapnel rained from the sky in burning meteors and plummeted back into the river, hissing as flames met water.

Nausea coursed through Maggie as she struggled to her feet, using the balcony to steady her. "That was a tourist boat," she said, recognizing the shape of the bow as it slowly submerged with what was left of the vessel.

The boat was gone. All those people... No one could have survived that.

Odd colored debris emerged from the water and bobbed among the sloshing waves. Maggie let out a cry when she realized what it was. Bile burned the back of her throat, and she covered her mouth to hold back the building scream.

The bodies, or what was left of them, floated like life-jackets among the wreckage.

Ashton wrapped an arm over Maggie's shoulder, his eyes glistening as they relived what happened in Trafalgar Square all over again. They'd failed, and all they could do was watch.

Sirens wailed in a mournful choir, emergency services narrowing in from all areas of the city. But their speed was in vain.

The damage was done.

***

Fifty-eight people. All of them dead.

Ashton handed Maggie a double whiskey with ice and plopped down on the couch beside her. They had returned to the apartment, leaving the French police and ambulances at the scene. It was a clean-up job now. There wasn't anything for them to do.

Maggie ran a hand through her hair, fingers still shaking.

Hakim betrayed them. He wasn't trying to take down Dabir. All of his crying and rage over his brother Khalid was bollocks, and Maggie let him lead her right up the garden path. He'd tricked her, and she fell for it like an amateur.

Now people were dead, and it was all her fault.

Maggie tossed back the amber liquid, and the sweet burn traveled down to her chest. The whiskey didn't fill her with its usual warmth, though. Inside she was bitter cold, frozen numb with the shock of everything she'd seen in the two attacks. Those kind of memories dug deep, like carvings etched in marble. They never went away. Not even when she closed her eyes to sleep.

She pulled the woolen throw closer to her chin and leaned her head on Ashton's shoulder. "I was a bloody idiot," she admonished, the guilt heavy as an anchor, weighing her down.

"*We* were bloody idiots you mean. We both let Hakim go, and I was the one who said I trusted him first." Ashton threw his empty glass into the roaring fire, which crackled and snapped as it consumed a pile of wood. The crystal glass shattered, and the pieces turned black as the flames licked over them.

Notre-Dame was a decoy. A very deliberate decoy chosen so Maggie and Ashton could witness the devastation of the Acolytes' latest hit.

"They wanted us to see it." They'd made sure to lead them on a wild goose chase across the city, positioning them with a front row seat to their heinous attack.

Ashton refilled Maggie's glass and drank a swig straight from the bottle. "No doubt. The sick fucks."

One minute, the tourists were enjoying a river cruise down the Seine, a perfect way to take in the Parisian sights with the interior of the boat offering warmth and drinks to sweeten the deal. The next minute, they were gone. Wiped from the earth in mere seconds.

The news played on mute in the background, and in the hours since, the death toll continued to rise. Passersby had been injured, too. An unfortunate few who were strolling by the banks of the river, or walking along the pavements above. Cars had crashed into each other in all the confusion, including one driver who had been hit with a piece of shrapnel that pierced through the windshield and killed her on impact.

The more they watched, the more Maggie and Ashton drank. It was self-pitying, she knew, but it was about all Maggie was capable of at that moment. There was only so much a person could take. Only so much death and destruction she could handle.

"Dabir and Hakim planned it all." Ashton glared at Dabir's note, which lay in front of them on the coffee table.

Maggie sipped her drink. "They could be long gone by now." So far, no video had surfaced of the Acolytes claiming the attack, but it was only a matter of time. Right now, they'd be celebrating, reeling with the high of executing another attack. This time right under their noses.

Hakim had given the French plenty of warning, yet they still managed to carry out their plans. His lies about trying to help, about giving them a clue to their next target, was utter bullshit. It had been a taunt. A boastful display of their confidence. And they'd been right. They attacked Paris unchecked, even with the advanced warning.

The Acolytes had delivered the world a message: they could destroy you, wherever and whenever they wanted, and nothing, not even the police or the government, could do anything to protect you from their wrath.

Maggie's phone rang, and Bishop's name popped up on the screen. She stared at it for a moment, the buzzing impatient and angry.

"Bishop," she said, waiting for the tirade to come. She put the phone on loudspeaker, Ashton staying silent as he listened.

"What happened?" Bishop asked, voice tight.

"My efforts failed." Maggie kept things succinct and to-the-point. "Dabir and his soldiers arranged a decoy explosive in the Notre-Dame cathedral, and I fell for it."

Maggie left out Hakim and his betrayal. She wasn't quite ready to discuss her foolishness with Bishop, to admit the complete incompetence she displayed in allowing a known terrorist to walk away from her grasp and return to his leader.

For all Maggie knew, Hakim had contacted Dabir the second he stepped into the electronics store and told him about her and Ashton. They could be the reason Dabir chose to act so quickly. Pushed to carry out the attack before she got close enough to stop them. Hakim's acting skills was enough to escape them once, but Dabir wouldn't risk a second meeting.

Bishop sighed over the phone, and Maggie pictured him pacing his office. "We've been tracking Dabir on our end to no avail. French intelligence haven't gotten anything substantial either."

"Has there been a video yet?" Maggie asked. If there were, the Unit would know about it long before the news channels did.

"No," Bishop said. "If they're following the pattern they carried out over here, they'll be moving on to their next location before releasing anything. I expect one will show up tomorrow."

"I'm sorry, Bishop."

"Are you hurt?" he asked, still concerned despite how she failed him. Failed everyone.

Her ribs ached from all the running, but she didn't complain. It was nothing compared to what the victims suffered. "No, I was far enough from the attack to avoid the blast." But close enough to see every second of it.

"Very well. Come home tomorrow. The director expects a full report in the afternoon. I don't need to warn you that she's in one hell of a mood."

Bishop didn't reprimand her or yell or shout. There was no need. He knew Maggie well enough to know she'd beat herself up enough for the both of them. Knew that nothing he said would be worse than what Maggie was telling herself.

"Okay," she said, not trusting herself to say much more. "I'll see you tomorrow then."

As soon as she hung up, Maggie burst into tears.

"Hey," Ashton said, pulling her into a hug. "It's all right, Mags."

"No, it's not." Maggie covered her face with her hands. Nothing was all right. It hadn't been for a long time now. "People are dead because of me."

"Those lives are not on you. They're on the Acolytes. Dabir and Hakim did this. You tried to stop them. You did what you could."

"But it wasn't good enough." The Acolytes could be anywhere now. Preparing for yet another attack, she couldn't prevent.

Ashton rubbed her back, his affection only leading her to cry more. "You can't blame yourself. You put yourself in harm's way to defuse what you thought was the bomb. You risked your life to do the right thing."

All the secrets Maggie had hidden from Ashton, all the private pain, bubbled up to the surface. She tried to push it back down, but the failure at the cathedral left her without any strength to fill the cracks in her mask. Her dam was about to burst, and she let it.

"Just before I left for that New York assignment, I found out I was pregnant."

The words spilled out, toppling from her lips. There was no taking them back. Ashton sat up and pulled off their blanket to look at her stomach.

"No," Maggie said, covering her flat tummy and unable to look at it. "I'm not anymore. I lost it. I lost my baby."

The last words came out in a wail, all pretense of strength gone. She couldn't keep it up any longer. Couldn't pretend that everything was fine and act like nothing had happened.

Ashton held her as she sobbed. She wasn't sure how long she wept. Too lost in the throes of her grief. Once she let the floodgates open, she didn't think the tears would ever stop.

They did, though. Eventually.

Ashton wiped her damp cheeks with the cuff of his sleeve, and Maggie saw her sadness reflected in his eyes. "Is, I mean, was Leon, the father?"

"Yes." Maggie stared at her hands. "But I haven't told him. How can I tell him?"

She couldn't bring herself to do it. To say the words out loud to him. To pass on the pain that had rampaged through her entire being since the doctor delivered the fatal news like a virus. Leon wouldn't take it well. Maggie knew him enough to know how much it would crush him. How much he'd always wanted a family.

"I knew something was up, but I had no idea." Ashton brushed her hair away from her face. "You could have told me. You don't need to go through this alone."

Maggie accepted the handkerchief Ashton offered and blew her nose. "I didn't want to think about it. If I told anyone else, I'd have to admit it really happened, that it wasn't just a terrible nightmare."

Maggie was good at running away from her problems. Detaching herself from reality and focusing on her missions. Playing the roles of her many aliases as if she was another person entirely. But there were some things you couldn't run from.

"When little Oliver died in my arms, it ripped open the wound again," she continued. "He was gone, just like my baby, and I couldn't do anything to save them. Just like I couldn't stop Dabir and Hakim today."

Maggie had been harsher than usual with Gabrielle Legrand. As much as the explosives dealer deserved what she got and more, it was unlike Maggie to resort to that level of violence based on a gut feeling that the woman was lying.

"I have this anger inside me. It's burning everything to ash, and I can't stop it. The Unit trained us to cope with all sorts of situations, but nothing prepared me for this. I was willing to change my entire life, Ash. I wanted my life to change. For a moment, I was going to be a mother. No fighting. No death. I was going to leave the Unit."

Ashton took her hands in his. "I can't imagine what you're going through. I'm sorry that happened to you."

"I suppose it wasn't meant to be," Maggie said, shaking her head. "Maybe I'm not cut out to be a mum, or have a normal life like everyone else."

"You can still have that normal life if you want it." Ashton eyes were intense, his dislike for the Unit burning even brighter than usual. "You can walk away whenever you want."

"I'm afraid that if I walked away, I'd have nothing left. I don't know if I could go through that again." Maggie laughed, but there was no humor in the sound. "And it's not like Leon, and I are this perfect, happy couple. Our fling in Venice shouldn't have happened. We know things will never work out between us. I couldn't even look him in the eye at the Unit briefing."

Seeing him, feeling his touch, had only solidified her decision not to tell Leon about the miscarriage. He didn't need to know.

"For what it's worth," Ashton said, reaching for a new glass in his little bar trolley by the couch. "I think you're going to be a brilliant wee mammy someday."

"You think?" Maggie asked, finishing off her latest double measure.

"Of course. Plus, I want some little nieces and nephews running around causing havoc."

Maggie allowed herself a small smile. "Uncle Ashton, eh?"

"Aye. And I'll apologize in advance for spoiling them rotten."

"No kids of your own then?" The topic of children didn't come up often since neither of them had any plans to start a family. Until she fell pregnant, Maggie hadn't allowed herself to consider it.

Ashton scoffed. "Are you kidding? I can barely look after myself."

Maggie actually laughed at that. Though the pain was still there, it wasn't quite as sharp with Ashton by her side.

"You'll get through this, you know," Ashton said, more confident than she was about the matter. "Just like you do everything else. And I'm here to help you in any way I can."

Maggie held out her empty glass. "Well in that case, how about you pour me another drink."

Ashton complied, and the TV caught Maggie's attention. The news carried on in the background, and an update flashed over the screen. Another victim had died in the hospital, bringing the death toll to fifty-nine.

"What are we going to do?" Ashton asked. As they watched, faces of confirmed victims appeared on the screen.

There wasn't much they *could* do. Maggie raised her glass, and they drank to the dead. She and Ashton sat there on the couch long into the night, until the fire had dimmed to embers, drowning their sorrows and drinking themselves into oblivion.

Chapter 9

---

31 December

Maggie stood over her friend, a glass of water and two painkillers in hand.

"Ashton."

It was still dark outside, the winter sun sleeping in late. Unlike Maggie. After a fitful few hours of sleep, she dragged herself out of bed, her troubled mind unable to rest.

"Ashton," she said louder this time, flicking on the light by his king-sized bed.

"What?" Ashton sat up, eyes still closed and his usually pristine hair suffering from a severe case of bedhead. "What's wrong?"

"Your phone."

Ashton rubbed the sleep from his eyes and peered up at her with a scrunched face. "Eh?"

"Your *phone*," Maggie repeated. "Is it registered in your name?"

"Come on, Mags. Nothing's in my real name."

"Good, then we can trace it." If the phone couldn't be linked back to Ashton, it was safe to have the Unit techs track it. If they asked any questions about the strange name of the owner, Maggie could say she stole it. They'd be too busy hunting the terrorists to ask much more than that.

"You want to go after the Acolytes?" Ashton asked, stretching his arms into the air and stifling a yawn. The tattoos covered both his arms in sleeves of black and grey, Maggie's favorite, a beautiful siren dragging an entranced sailor down into the depths of the ocean, catching her eye.

"We're going to find them," Maggie vowed.

"They could be anywhere by now."

"Then we'll hunt them down." Maggie would follow them to the ends of the earth if that's what it took. They were not slipping away from her that easily. She handed the water and tablets to Ashton. "Take these. Coffee's brewing as we speak."

Ashton was useless without caffeine in his system, and she needed him at his best.

"What if Hakim tossed the phone?" Ashton asked. "He'll know we can trace it, too."

The thought had occurred to Maggie earlier, as the beginnings of her plan stewed in her mind. It was a long shot, but she had to try something. She wasn't prepared to give up. Not after everything the Acolytes had done. They didn't get to walk away from this.

"Right now, it's all we've got. Now get ready. Please," she said, checking her watch. "I want to be out of here within the hour."

Maggie was already dressed and ready to go. Her cold shower and painkillers were enough to sober her from last night's whiskey. The time for feeling sorry for herself was over. The victims of the attacks deserved vengeance, and Maggie intended to get it for them.

Ashton didn't protest. He rolled out of bed and padded across the room to open the drapes in nothing but his birthday suit. "Don't you have to report to crabbit old Helmsley this afternoon?"

Maggie may have made a mistake with Hakim, but she wouldn't be fooled a second time. She wasn't returning home until she righted her blunder and put an end to the Acolytes. She was out for blood, and this time it was personal.

"The director will have to wait." Maggie tossed Ashton his clothes. "We've got terrorists to catch."

Twenty minutes and three espressos later, Maggie and Ashton were in her rental. Ashton drove while Maggie called in the trace.

It didn't take long for the techs to hack into the phone's network provider and find an address. Like Maggie, they had been trained to be the best in their respective field and could cause as much damage with their keyboards as Maggie could with her fists.

"Thanks, Gregg. Say hello to Liz for me." Maggie hung up and typed the address into the Sat-Nav, anticipation building inside her like sparks of electricity. "They're still in Paris."

Ashton checked the directions and took a right turn. "Is that a good thing or a bad thing?"

Maggie stared out the window at the unrelenting snow. "I guess we'll find out."

Their destination in Belleville was only six miles from Ashton's place, but it took them a full forty minutes to get there. The snow made the traffic worse than usual, and Ashton drove an extra five minutes out of the way to avoid the Rue de Rivoli. Maggie didn't complain. She didn't want to pass the spot of yesterday's disaster.

A somber tone had befallen the city. Parisian's were resilient though, and this wasn't the first time they'd found themselves the targets of hate. Already people were gathering with signs of love and solidarity, heading to the Arc de Triomphe where the news showed a growing crowd coming out in the cold to be together during their time of sorrow.

Ashton parked a safe distance away from the phone's location and reversed into a graffiti-covered alleyway. They got out of the car, and Maggie had them recheck their weapons. She carried her knives, gun, and an extra magazine in case things got messy.

Other than pickpockets, Belleville was relatively safe during the day when hipsters opened their boutique coffee shops and secondhand clothing stores. It was at night when the shutters closed that a very different type of vendor took over. Drug dealing and prostitution generally made the neighborhood a place to avoid, especially the narrow side streets.

The butcher's shop rested at the end of a dead-end street and took up the entire building. Like the rest of the surrounding stores, it was closed for the day and darkness lay beyond the windows. Deals were written on the glass in French and Arabic, offering the usual items as well as halāl ready cold cuts and rotisserie chickens.

Maggie motioned for Ashton to follow her around the back, and they crept along the building's walls, keeping an eye out for scouts or spies. A butcher's shop wasn't what Maggie expected, but she trusted the techs were correct with the location.

Someone had threaded a heavy chain through the metal double doors, the lock new and well-oiled. Even if Maggie and Ashton could pick the lock, a parked van blocked their access to the entry. The windows at this end of the building were narrow and frosted, too, giving no hint of what lay inside. Ashton tapped Maggie's shoulder and pointed above them.

A raised skylight protruded from the slanted roof, a ground level section that connected to the main two-story building that housed the shop floor. With a silent nod, they hoisted themselves onto a large dumpster and shimmied up to the roof with the help of a drainpipe.

Maggie rolled on top and waited for Ashton before crawling to the corner of the skylight. Snow melted under the heat of her body and soaked into her clothes, layers of grime covering her jacket and trousers as she slid across to get a look inside.

The snow covered the skylight glass too, and Maggie risked wiping a small section away to peek inside. Shadows lingered across the floor, odd shapes that didn't make sense until she swiped away more snow. Animal carcasses hung on hooks, their bodies stripped and flayed, ready to be sliced and diced into cuts of meat. The animals lined in macabre rows of red muscle and sinew.

The animal bodies weren't alone, though. Maggie recognized the two men from Notre-Dame standing between the rows, speaking with someone. Muffled voices emanated from within and Maggie pressed her ear against the glass pane, making room for Ashton to get a glimpse inside.

The slap of a fist meeting flesh echoed in the chilled chamber.

"Stop it, Assad. Dabir wants him alive." The white man grabbed his partner and shoved him back before returning his attention to the person sitting before them. Maggie sucked in a gasp when she saw who it was.

Hakim.

The white guy grabbed Hakim's face in his meaty hand. "Dabir wants to kill you himself. Streaming live online for everyone to see. The world will learn what happens when you betray your Brothers."

Blood oozed from Hakim's nostrils, his nose swollen like the rest of his face. Garish purple bruises replaced the bags under his eyes, the surrounding white one of his irises turned red and bloodshot.

Betrayed?

Maggie shared a look with Ashton as they listened on.

"I only have one brother," Hakim said, tied to a chair much the same as he had been when he was in Maggie's detainment.

Hakim's resistance earned him another blow, this one to his gut.

"You aren't half the man Khalid was. *We* were his Brothers. He wouldn't acknowledge someone as weak as you."

"Khalid fell for the same self-righteous crap you both did. You're nothing but a bunch of fanatics, man. Allah wouldn't want this. Dabir has you all fooled."

That earned him two blows, this time from Assad. Hakim took them without crying out, though he couldn't hide the pain from his face.

"You can shit talk all you want," said Assad, "but we're not going to stop until you tell us who you're in contact with. Who were you trying to warn about yesterday's attack?"

Hakim titled his head back and let out a sardonic laugh.

Maggie knew that laugh. Had bellowed it herself a few times when the chips were down. It was the laugh of someone who had resigned themselves to death. The Acolytes wouldn't let him live now that he'd betrayed them, and Hakim knew it. Keeping the truth from them was his last rebellious act. The only piece of power he had left.

She closed her eyes. Hakim hadn't lied to them. He'd been found out.

A wash of relief came over her, selfish as it was. She hadn't been wrong to trust Hakim. His plan to infiltrate the Acolytes had been true enough. Only Dabir and the others had caught him in the act before he could contact Maggie.

"What's the plan?" Ashton asked in her ear, coming to the same conclusion.

Maggie thought it over, weighing the options to achieve the cleanest outcome. They couldn't let him stay there much longer. Assad and the other guy were quickly running out of patience with him. "I'll cause a distraction. When the room is clear, break in and get Hakim out."

Ashton nodded, and Maggie maneuvered to the edge of the roof and slipped back down.

Returning to the front of the shop, Maggie risked checking inside, cupping her hands to get a better look. She didn't see anyone else inside. A pit of unease burned in her stomach. Where were the other Acolytes?

Maggie gave herself a shake and focused on the task at hand. A bike sat chained up against a railing a few shops down. It likely belonged to the resident in the flat above. She used one of her many knives, picking the lock without much trouble, and wheeled the bike over to the butcher's shop.

She had been trained in the delicate art of breaking and entering. Taught how to pick locks and slip into even the most rigorously guarded fortresses. To sneak around unnoticed and leave without a single trace of her presence. Silent. Cautious.

Now wasn't one of those times.

Hoisting the bike up over her head, Maggie lurched back and threw it with everything she had. Her ribs protested the movement, but her aim was true.

The bike soared through the air and crashed into the front window in a cacophony of shattered glass. The windowpane clung to shards of glittering glass, giving her improvised entrance the look of a gaping mouth with jagged teeth.

Maggie stepped into the store with a knife in each hand, glass crunching under her boots. No alarm went off, but she'd made enough racket to draw the wanted attention. Quick footsteps drew near, coming from the back.

Assad bounded through the door a second later, wide shoulders barely fitting between the frame, and spotted her. Maggie sent one of her knives spinning through the air.

The blade closed the distance between them and imbedded itself into Assad's chest. He stared down at the hilt and blinked twice before crumpling to the ground with a massive *thump*.

A second set of footsteps grew louder, Assad's partner falling for her trap. Maggie crossed the room and pressed her back against the wall by the door as she waited for him, crouched down on the balls of her feet.

Maggie let him thunder into the room and see his fallen Brother. Then, lashing out with her second blade, she sliced, deep and precise across the backs of his ankles.

Blood spurted from the cut flesh. The big oaf dropped to his knees and screamed as the pain of his butchered tendons registered.

The screams were short lived. Maggie lunged onto his back and slit his throat with vicious efficiency.

She didn't wait to watch him die. It wouldn't take long for someone to call the police, and they'd already be on high alert after yesterday. Ashton met her in the back, more glass covering the floor from his own makeshift entrance from the skylight.

Hakim looked even worse up close.

"How did you find me?" he asked as Ashton freed him from the chair.

"Ashton's phone," Maggie said, keeping an eye out by the door for any unwanted arrivals.

Hakim groaned as he got to his feet. "They took it off me in the van on the way here yesterday morning." The van that was left parked out back, which was just as well for Hakim. Not so good for Assad and his friend, though. "Dabir text you the wrong location for the bomb right in front of me."

"Where's Dabir and the rest of the Acolytes now?" Ashton asked as he helped lead Hakim to the door. Maggie walked in front of them, primed and ready for any surprises.

"I heard Ben and Assad talking," said Hakim, his grave tone making Maggie stop and turn around to face him. "Dabir's going to attack the city again. Tonight."

Maggie's heart plummeted. "Where?"

"The Champs-Élysées."

Chapter 10

Maggie stomped around Ashton's living room with her phone pressed against her ear.

"Are you fucking kidding me?"

"They're not bending on it." Bishop sighed, and Maggie pictured him running a hand down his face. "If they move people away from the Champs-Élysées, or try to evacuate the city, it would only show the Acolytes that they'd won."

Maggie was all for showing no fear in the face of adversity, especially against those whose aim was to instill terror in the hearts of people, but things were getting serious now. Deadly.

"Bloody French," she muttered. They were almost as stubborn as the British.

Maggie watched the news coverage, reporters coming in live from the scene as what looked like half the city congregated on the famous street, clustering around at the Arc de Triumphe.

"They're on high alert and have as many people on the ground as they can," Bishop said.

Maggie had called in the news to Bishop, bringing him up to speed about Hakim's true motives and Dabir's plans for an impending attack. "They were on high alert yesterday, but Dabir still succeeded. What's going to stop him from doing it again this time?"

"They have the location this time," Bishop replied, though he didn't sound convinced.

Maggie sat down at the dinner table where Hakim devoured a bowl of soup and bread. She tapped her fingers on the wood. The past few hours of phone calls and waiting grated on her nerves. "I still don't like it. I'm going to make sure I'm there. I don't trust anyone else with this."

"Be careful," Bishop warned. She'd barely escaped two bombings now and, if what Hakim said was true, Dabir was planning quite the bang with his third.

"I'll try," she said with a deep sigh. "Call me with any updates." Maggie tossed the phone on the table and rubbed her aching head.

"They're not moving them, are they?" Hakim asked. After a hot shower and some new clothes, he looked a bit better than how they found him. Still, his so-called Brothers Ben and Assad had done a number on him. One of the cuts on his cheek needed stitches, and Ashton had to dig out the first aid kit. Hakim was stronger than he looked though, accepting the stitches without a fuss.

"No, they're not," Maggie said, topping up on her painkillers. Her ribs hadn't fared well with all the climbing and killing at the butcher's shop, but she couldn't sit back and rest now.

The Champs-Élysées was flooded with people. No police detail could be one hundred percent vigilant with a crowd like that. The tourists would provide more than enough cover for Dabir and the Acolytes to go unnoticed. Maggie needed to be on the ground.

"What are we going to do?" Hakim asked, chewing on a bread roll. The Acolytes hadn't given him so much as a sip of water since yesterday, and he was making up for it now, already on this third bowl of soup.

"*We* aren't doing anything," Maggie corrected. "You've done enough."

More than enough. Not many people Hakim's age had the guts or the cunning to infiltrate a terrorist organization. He'd spent almost a year with the ones who brainwashed his brother, never losing sight of his craving for vengeance. It couldn't have been easy.

"But –"

"But nothing," Ashton said calmly, coming in with two steaming cups of tea for them both. "You'll stay here until we get back."

Hakim's face grew sullen, and he swirled his spoon in his soup instead of meeting their eyes. "Let me help. I messed up yesterday. Because of me, more people are dead."

"That's not on you," Maggie said, echoing Ashton's words to her the night before. She refrained from reaching out and placing a hand on his shoulder, afraid that it would hurt after Ben and Assad's handiwork. "Dabir is to blame for this, and I'm going to make sure he pays for it."

Ashton sat down next to Hakim. "We wouldn't know anything if it wasn't for you. It took guts to do what you did."

Maggie agreed. If Bishop were there, he'd already be sizing up Hakim as a possible candidate for agent training. His intellect and evident skills in infiltration would make him very appealing to the Unit.

Maggie reached out and squeezed his hand. "Let us use your intel to end this."

Hakim gave a short nod. He appeared less than happy about being left out, but he ducked his head and went back to his meal without comment.

"Any word on our friend Gabrielle?" Ashton asked.

Maggie sipped her tea before she spilled the only good news Bishop had for her. "She's been charged with enough offenses to keep a judge very busy. The French plan to make an example of her."

Ashton grinned at that. "She's going to hate those prison jumpsuits." His face sobered when he looked over Maggie's shoulder and out to the city beyond. "There should be fireworks in the sky by now."

Given recent events, the police had canceled the traditional New Year's Eve fireworks and banned the use of private displays as well. They'd already received an overwhelming number of frightened calls, scared Parisians reporting sounds of an explosion or shifty strangers roaming in their neighborhoods. The city had accepted the request, leaving the night sky dark and untouched.

The Eifel tower across the river should be twinkling like a Christmas tree, too. Instead, it stood tall and unlit in mournful remembrance to yesterday's victims.

"Come on," Maggie said, gulping down the rest of her tea. "It's time we head out."

Dabir was out there somewhere, and Maggie was going to find him.

Chapter 11

The Champs-Élysées was the place to be on New Year's Eve. An annual grand parade marched down the length of the famous street culminating in a magnificent light show at the Arc de Triomphe to usher in the new year.

It was a different story this year.

The parade had been canceled, and in its place, a small vigil had grown into a mass gathering of mourners coming to pay their respects to those who'd lost their lives. The Arc de Triomphe served as a central altar, its light show changed to display the names of each of the confirmed victims instead of wishing everyone a *Bonne Année.*

As Maggie searched for the Acolytes, a sea of candles bathed placards and handmade signs in soft light. Some were commemorative, others angry or political. All displayed the unrelenting strength of Paris. Times may be hard, but they would stand tall and carry on.

Maggie shook her head and gestured out to the crowd. "This is impossible, Ash. All Dabir and the Acolytes need to do is mask as mourners. We'll never be able to pick them out in this."

They'd been there for hours now and had completed several sweeps through the crowd to no avail.

Ashton dropped his binoculars and nudged his head over to a nearby woman standing guard with an assault rifle. "Maybe those lot scared them off."

The French government had brought in military reinforcements to help contain the situation. Most wore their uniforms as an outward show of their presence. There were groups dressed as civilians, too, dispersed throughout the crowd. Dabir wasn't an idiot, though. He would have planned for the increase in security.

"No, he's here somewhere." Maggie felt it in her gut. According to Hakim, destroying the boat hardly made a dent in the truckload of explosives Dabir had acquired from Legrand. The Acolytes retained more than enough power to obliterate the entire vicinity and everyone in it.

"We should go," Ashton said. "You'll drive yourself nuts waiting here."

Ashton was right, but weaving through the crowd wasn't going to help. Dabir was a strategist. Based on the previous attacks, his plans were airtight. Nearly impossible to stop.

"We need to think." Maggie massaged her aching forehead and tried to concentrate. "Hakim said they had a shitload of explosives, right? Dabir would need someplace to conceal them."

There were plenty of buildings lining the street, but the police had already checked most of them. While Dabir and his followers could hide in plain sight, that volume of explosives would be harder to hide.

"Wherever they are, we need to find them quick. It's forty minutes to midnight." Ashton shifted on his feet, the anticipation of disaster putting them both on edge. And they weren't the only ones. Tension made the police fidget and the soldiers stand with especially rigid postures. They'd all been briefed; they all knew what was coming.

Maggie had to stop it. "You think he's waiting until the bells ring?"

"Looks like it. He certainly has an air for dramatics."

"Yes," Maggie agreed, thinking of the first attack back home.

Nina and Leon had spoken about the symbolism of hitting London's heart. The Arc de Triomphe de l'Étoile lay in the center of the Place Charles de Gaulle, a large road junction with twelve radiating avenues, hence the name: Triumphal Arch of the Star. It was the pinnacle of French patriotism, there to commemorate fallen soldiers, with an eternal flame burning for the unidentified who had died in the wars.

"Wait, that's it." Maggie grabbed Ashton's arm and yanked him down the stairs.

"What?"

Maggie pushed and shoved her way through the thicket of people, ignoring their protests as she headed straight for the opposite end of the Arc de Triomphe. "Dabir used the underground to plant his bomb below Trafalgar Square. What if he's done the same here?"

Ashton's gaze slipped to the ground as he kept pace beside her. Acknowledgment lit his eyes. "The underpass."

Maggie nodded and charged forward. If Ashton was right about the bomb going off at midnight, they had no time to politely travel between the huddles of people.

An underpass tunnel lay at the Avenue de la Grande Armee side of the circle, directly opposite the Champs-Élysées. It gave pedestrians a safe way to cross the round-about and reach the Arc de Triomphe without risking their lives crossing the notorious road that circled it. With no road marks and traffic coming from the twelve encompassing boulevards, attempts to cross the road were as good as suicide.

Thanks to the crowd, Maggie and Ashton had no vehicle traffic to worry about. When they finally reached the entrance to the pass, they took the steps leading down to the opening two at a time.

"Maggie! Ashton!" came a voice behind them. "Hey, Maggie, wait."

Maggie spun on her heels. "Hakim? What are you doing here?"

"We told you to stay in the apartment," Ashton yelled.

Hakim descended the steps to reach them, limping and favoring his right leg. "I know, but I was watching the coverage on the TV, and it came to me. Dabir's going to do what he did at—"

"Trafalgar Square. Yes, we know," Maggie said.

Hakim deflated. "Oh."

Ashton checked his watch, panic in his voice. "Thirty-five minutes left, Mags."

"Go back to Ashton's, and be quick about it," Maggie ordered. "If we're right, the bomb's about to go off at midnight."

Hakim raised his chin and continued down the stairs. "I'm coming with you. This is my fight as much as yours."

Maggie didn't have time to argue. Time was ticking, and each second she wasted could mean the death of thousands. "Fine, but stay behind us. If things get bad, I want you to get out of there, okay?"

"Yeah, no heroics," Ashton said, handing Hakim one of his guns. "If we tell you to run, you run."

Hakim cocked the gun and gave a firm nod. "Fine."

It seemed Hakim hadn't wasted his time with the Acolytes. Bishop really would be interested in recruiting the boy. They set off without another word, keeping close.

Their pounding footsteps echoed off the walls, the ceiling arched and low to the ground. Shadows splayed out showing their approach thanks to the brightness of the lights that shone off the cream tiles.

"There," Maggie said, pointing to a jut in the wall: a service door lined within the tiles, its discreet handle the only thing indicating its presence.

Ashton grabbed the handle, and Maggie stood with her gun at the ready. The door had only opened a crack when it swung open from the inside.

An Acolyte barged though, the door hitting Ashton and knocking him back. The man charged straight for Hakim, but Maggie was ready for him. She shot him point blank in the back of the head and sent his brains splattering against the wall.

The gunshot reverberated through the tunnel. So much for the element of surprise.

The man's presence at least confirmed they were right about Dabir going underground. Motioning with a wave, Maggie took the helm and led her small team into the darkness beyond the door.

There were no lights here, and Maggie waited for her eyes to adjust before venturing too far in. Where there was one Acolyte, more would follow. "How many Brothers are left?" she asked Hakim, keeping her voice to a whisper.

"Eight," Hakim said from behind Ashton. "Nine if Dabir's here."

"Oh, he's here all right," Maggie said. He wouldn't want to miss his grand finale.

The narrow pathway was only wide enough for two

people, the surrounding walls bare and bitter cold to the touch.

Ashton rummaged in his pocket and brought out a small flashlight. It flickered to life and illuminated the faces of two approaching Acolytes.

Afraid to fire in such close proximity, Maggie holstered her gun, reached for her knives, and dove forward.

Maggie collided with the first man, knocking him to the ground and pinning him down. Her ribs screamed with pain, but she couldn't let up without losing her advantage. Ashton and Hakim were busy with the second attacker, the flashlight clattering to the ground with a crack. The light blinked out, and Maggie battled blind, aiming to stab the man beneath her.

Her opponent caught Maggie's wrist before the blade could penetrate. The Acolyte tried to pivot under her, but Maggie squeezed her thighs against the brute's sides and held steady.

Both their hands shook as they struggled. The man was stronger than Maggie, but she had the better position. She pushed with all her might, and he gasped as the tip of Maggie's knife met his flesh.

He wriggled under her, adrenaline giving his superior strength the edge it needed to push the blade back out. Maggie's arms shook, but she couldn't let him turn the blade. If he did, the tides would turn. She tightened her grip and dropped forward, pushing her entire weight into the hilt.

For a second, nothing happened. The blade quivered in the open air between them. Then the man sucked in a breath as his strength failed him and the knife plunged into his chest, glancing off his ribcage.

Warmth coated her hands, and a single sigh marked his final breath.

Sliding out her blade, Maggie got to her feet and wiped the slick blood onto her trousers.

"You good?" Ashton asked as he and Hakim came into view.

"Yes," Maggie said, catching her breath. "You?"

"Two down," Hakim reported. "Seven to go."

A shuffle of feet caught in Maggie's ear, and she spun in time to grab an approaching Brother. Maggie twisted away from his grabbing arms and caught him in a headlock.

His fingernails dug into her jacket, but she didn't relent. Then, with a vicious snap, she twisted his head and let his convulsing body fall to the floor.

"Make that six."

Hakim blinked in astonishment. "Wow."

Conscious of the literal ticking clock, Maggie ventured further down the pathway. A screeching noise rumbled beyond the walls, and the floor vibrated under their feet. It whizzed past them in a rush of sound and carried off into the distance.

"The Métro," Maggie explained to Ashton and Hakim. It must have been a train passing on the Charles de Gaulle – Étoile line that passed underneath the Arc de Triomphe.

The pathway grew wider, and after thirty more feet or so, it opened out into a generator room. Voices echoed from further down, but the noises coming from the Métro lines stopped them from being clear.

But Maggie knew who the voices belonged to, no matter the muffled sounds. She inched closer to the end of the pathway's wall.

Glancing back at Ashton and Hakim, who nodded their assent, Maggie rearmed herself and darted into the room.

Chapter 12

Everything happened in a flurry of bright flashes.

As soon as Maggie came into view, five Brothers holding guns released a tirade of bullets in her direction.

She lunged to the ground, ducking behind a piece of machinery and skinning her palms on the landing.

Ashton and Hakim made the most of the distraction and charged after her, gunshots deafening as bullets ricocheted off the metal shells of the generators.

Springing back up, Maggie swung out from the other side of the machinery and fired. The first bullet clipped an Acolyte in the shoulder. He fell back, but not before she planted another bullet in his chest.

A second body fell at Maggie's feet, and she turned to see a grinning Hakim lowering his gun. He shot her a wink before another Acolyte aimed at him, and he ducked out of the way.

Maggie followed suit and pressed against one of the machines. Risking a look, she spotted Dabir heading towards a door at the far end of the room.

"Oh no, you don't."

Leaping over a dead Acolyte, Maggie aimed fire. Dabir moved at the last minute, and the bullets imbedded in the door with a clang.

The terrorist leader abandoned the exit and dodged out of sight. Maggie made to follow him, but an Acolyte grabbed her from the back. He yanked her hair, and Maggie hissed as her blond locks tore from her scalp.

Maggie lashed out and caught him with a fist to the face. In his shock and pain, Maggie wriggled free and disarmed the gun from his hands.

The Acolyte recovered quick. He dodged her next punch and spun, kicking Maggie in her already broken ribs.

Acute pains stabbed up her side, and she doubled over. The Acolyte caught her with an uppercut and sent her flying back, her gun slipping from her grip and skidding across the floor.

Ashton's screams echoed through the room, and Maggie's stomach lurched. She gazed over at the exit door from on her back, dizzy with the throbbing pain in her ribs. Ashton was grappling with one of the terrorists, blood running down his face.

A fist caught Maggie across the jaw, forcing her attention back to her own opponent. She reached into her jacket and lashed out with the knife concealed there, slicing the blade through the air as the Acolyte swung again.

He pulled his fist back and roared in anger. Maggie jumped to her feet, and they circled the floor. She feinted an attack, but he didn't fall for it, holding back to avoid the edge of her blade.

Every move Maggie made sent shooting pains across her ribs. She went for another attack, but the Acolyte dodged and came in with one of his own.

The kick was hard, and Maggie was too slow to block it. It caught her in the ribs again, and fear thundered in her chest as she let out another cry of pain. The Acolyte knew she was injured. Knew her weak points.

Nausea coursed through Maggie, and she barely refrained from retching, forcing down bile as she stumbled to get back up. Hands reached out for her, and at first, she thought it was her opponent.

Only when her original opponent returned did Maggie realize one of his Brothers had arrived to help end her life.

Still clutching to her knife, Maggie squirmed out of the new attacker's grip and brought her knife down on his boot. The newly sharpened blade made light work of the leather, and Maggie gave the knife a savage twist once it was in his foot.

Her original opponent grabbed her hair again and pulled her away from his Brother. Maggie let him drag her up, still holding onto her blade. A spray of blood covered her face from the second man's sliced foot, and she swung the knife up, using the momentum the first man provided.

Maggie roared and lodged the knife under the first Acolyte's chin. The blade went right through the skin, and the glint of metal winked at her as the Acolyte opened his mouth in shock.

His hold on her loosened. Maggie pulled out the knife and shoved the Acolyte back. He toppled over, and she left him to bleed out while she dealt with his Brother.

The second Acolyte was still holding his foot. Maggie jammed her knife in his back, the blade slicing through his spine.

He wasn't too fussed about his foot after that.

A gunshot rang out behind her, and Maggie's heart hammered in her ears. Her mind went to Ashton, and she raced for the door, afraid she'd find him bleeding out. Instead, she found him standing over another dead Acolyte. He checked his gun and, finding the clip empty, tossed it to the ground.

From her count, all of the Acolytes were down, except for one. "Where's Dabir?" she asked Ashton, giving him a quick check for wounds requiring immediate attention. Like her, he hadn't come out unscathed, but the cut on his head appeared superficial.

"I see you brought your friends, Hakim."

Maggie and Ashton snapped their heads towards the voice and found Dabir stepping out from one of the generators. He held Hakim at gunpoint, using him as a shield as he inched towards the middle of the room.

"Dabir," Maggie growled. She and Ashton spread out, angling in on the last living member of the Acolytes of the Holy War.

"Don't come any closer," he warned, pressing the end of the gun into Hakim's temple.

"Shoot him," Hakim spat, his words strangled by Dabir's muscled arm locked around his throat.

Maggie reached for her weapon, but she'd lost it during the fighting. She eyed the pile of explosives behind Dabir and Hakim, packed like a crate of bricks and wired to a detonator. A timer sat on top, running down the minutes, second by second.

"I would've preferred to be long gone before the main event, but you leave me no choice." Dabir followed Maggie's alarmed gaze to the wired device and punched in a series of numbers, his gun still trained on Hakim.

The timer went from twenty-nine minutes remaining to five.

A train rushed by through the walls, likely the very one Dabir and his men had planned to catch to make a quick exit before time ran out on the bomb, giving them a full half hour to escape to safety.

Maggie inched cautiously forward, arms held out.

"Dabir, it isn't too late. You can stop the bomb. You don't need to die down here."

Four minutes and twenty seconds.

"Foolish bitch. You think you can talk your way out of this? I'm not afraid to die. I'll be treated as a king in the afterlife, rewarded for my services to Allah."

"You're going to Jahannam," Hakim rasped, condemning Dabir to hell. "Allah will see you punished for the lives you've taken. There's no place in paradise for people like you."

Maggie stared at the timer.

Three minutes and forty-nine seconds.

Dabir reached behind him with his gun hand and grabbed something from the pile of explosives. "I guess we'll find out."

It was a detonator.

Maggie and Ashton moved to stop him, but they were too far away. Until now, Maggie had been afraid to throw her knife in case it hit Hakim, but it was a risk she'd need to take.

Dabir's thumb reached out to press down on the detonator, ready to manually override the timer and set the bomb off three minutes early.

"No!" Hakim cried. He bit down on Dabir's arm as Maggie threw her blade.

Dabir jerked back, shaking off Hakim's attack, inadvertently saving himself from taking Maggie's knife to the face.

Free from Dabir's clutches, Hakim dropped down next to a fallen Acolyte and took the gun he held in his dead hands. Dabir saw what Hakim was doing and aimed his weapon at the boy, dropping the detonator in the process.

Two guns fired.

But only one bullet found its target.

Chapter 13

Hakim's gun slipped through his fingers.

"No!" Maggie screamed. Hakim's eyes widened as he held a hand against his chest. His fingers came back wet and dripping red.

Hakim missed the shot, but Dabir hadn't.

Ashton ran to Hakim's side, but Maggie only had eyes for Dabir, a blast of fury igniting within her.

Dabir's maniacal laughter boomed through the room, and he returned his attention to the detonator.

Maggie dove, hitting the ground in a roll. On the way back to her feet, she grabbed Hakim's fallen gun and released three rapid shots.

The bullets reached their intended target, and Maggie smirked in dark satisfaction to see each of the deliberately placed holes in the terrorist's body.

Dabir's right hand no longer held the detonator, the device falling to his feet. In fact, his right hand ceased to exist. All that was left was a bloody, torn mess. The oozing hole in his chest mirrored the one in his forehead, and Dabir was dead by the time his body collapsed to the ground.

Maggie lowered her gun but didn't stop to process what happened.

She returned to her team, the rising panic clear in her voice. "Ashton." She pulled her friend up from Hakim as the boy lay on the floor with blood pooling around him. "Ashton, the bomb!"

Ashton stumbled to his feet, the blood draining from his face as Maggie led him to the pack of explosives.

Two minutes and thirty-one seconds.

They were all going to die.

"Can you stop it?" Maggie asked, shaking Ashton by the shoulders when he wouldn't respond, shock leaving him still as marble.

Ashton blinked once. Twice. Then with a shake of his head, he was himself again. He examined the bomb, each passing second bringing them closer to death. Wires jutted out and wrapped around the explosives in all directions, each of them a different color.

Maggie knew enough about bombs to know not all of them were necessary, placed there to confuse anyone trying to defuse it. One wrong cut of a decoy wire and the thing would blow instantly.

"Give me a knife," Ashton said, picking through the wires with blood-soaked hands.

Maggie complied, handing him the one strapped to her ankle. "Do you know which wire to cut?"

"I'm not sure."

"You have to be sure. Or we and the thousands of people above us are going to be obliterated."

Ashton mopped his brow and let out a hollow laugh. "No pressure then."

Maggie paced behind him, trying not to add to his nerves, but they were running out of time. "Fifty seconds, Ash."

"I know, I know." Ashton fumbled with the wires, tracing them along their winding course around the explosives.

Forty seconds.

"It's between the blue one and the green," Ashton announced, his brow furrowed in concentration.

Maggie stood beside him, her mind turning to thoughts of Leon, and if she would ever get to see him again. "Which is it?"

"I don't know."

Thirty seconds.

"Hurry, Ashton. It's going to blow!"

Ashton let out a shaky breath, the knife in his hand hovering next to the green wire.

Twenty seconds.

"Do it!" Maggie urged, her muscles tightening as she

prepared for the worst.

Ashton went to cut the green, but at the last moment, he switched and grabbed the blue, pulling the knife up and snapping the wire in two.

The timer read eleven seconds and stayed there.

Maggie and Ashton stared at the clock. The seconds ticked on, but the clock didn't move. Finally, the tension melted out of Maggie's shoulders as their victory settled in.

"How did you know it was the blue wire?" Maggie leaned against the wall, her body going limp as her muscles relaxed, overcome with relief.

Ashton shrugged. "I didn't."

Maggie started, eyes wide and mouth agape. "You guessed?"

"Life's a gamble, Mags," Ashton said like he just bet money on black or red at a roulette table instead of gambling the lives of thousands of people on a whim.

Maggie couldn't help but laugh. She shoved Ashton back a step then pulled him into her in a bear hug, not caring about the pain it caused her aching ribs. Blue was definitely her new favorite color.

They released each other and let out a triumphant sigh. They'd done it. They saved everyone. Maggie turned back to Hakim.

Well, almost everyone.

Maggie knelt down beside her old target.

"You did it," he said, staring up at them.

"We did it," Maggie corrected and took his hand with a squeeze. Ashton helped her bring him up to a sitting position.

Hakim smiled, his teeth stained red from the blood filling his mouth. "I'm glad you found me when you did. I couldn't have taken out Dabir on my own."

Maggie bit back tears and waited until she trusted herself to reply. "Thousands of people are alive because of you." Without Hakim, they would have never have found Dabir. His reign of terror would have continued with disastrous results.

"I'm going to die, aren't I?" Hakim asked.

He had already lost too much blood. There wasn't enough time to get him help, and Maggie couldn't lie to him. Not after everything he'd been through. He deserved the truth. "Yes."

A tear slid down his face as he accepted his fate, brave as ever. "Can you guys do something for me?"

"Anything," Ashton said, wiping at his eyes.

Hakim gave them his last request, and Maggie took out her phone.

It didn't take long after that. They stayed with him, Ashton cracking jokes all the while to distract him from the pain. His breathing grew weak, and Maggie stroked his hair, holding him, just as she had held little Oliver only days before.

Hakim finally slipped away in her arms, the light going out from those fiery, determined eyes of his. Maggie closed them shut and bowed her head over his body.

He was gone.

Chapter 14

LONDON, GREAT BRITAIN
2 JANUARY

Maggie brushed the hair from her bruised face as the wind picked up across the graveyard. She stood at the top of the hill, watching the mourners below say their final farewells to Oliver Clark and his mum, Anna.

The city had come out in support, touched and saddened by the story of the little boy and his young mother who had died at the hands of the now eliminated terrorists. Or at least, Dabir's branch of the organization. Groups like the Acolytes were like the mythical hydra. You chopped off one head, and two more grew in its place.

Maggie hadn't attended the church service. People were lined all the way outside and around the church gardens for the Clarks. Part of her was glad so many people cared for Oliver and Anna, and another part was relieved there wasn't room for her in the church. She didn't think she could have made it through the whole ceremony.

Maggie hugged herself against the cold as the snow continued to fall, cradling an absent hand over her stomach. Her ribs were in the process of healing; the Acolyte she'd fought added an extra break to the existing two. Still, she bore the pain. Pain meant she was alive.

The Clark funeral was one of many to take place over the last few days as the victims of the Trafalgar Square attack were laid to rest. The French were currently in the process of making sure all the bodies of the tourists on the Seine riverboat made it home so their friends and family could say a proper goodbye. It wasn't possible for all, given the nature of the attack.

"Thought I'd find you here."

Ashton walked over to her, and they stood shoulder to shoulder as they watched Oliver's tiny coffin being laid into the ground. Maggie knew he'd come, even if he hadn't expected to find her there. Though he tried to mask it behind his usual care-free front, the last week had taken as much of a toll on him as it had her.

"You okay?" she asked.

"Aye," he lied. "You?"

Maggie leaned her head into his shoulder. "Yeah."

"Look at this." Ashton handed his new phone to her. "Our boy Hakim's gone viral."

Hakim's beaten face appeared on the screen, the image jarring. Her heart panged at the sight of him, and she made a mental note to ask Bishop for Hakim's mother's address. She deserved to know how brave her youngest son had been from someone who had been there with him. While it wouldn't bring her son back, Maggie hoped it would give her some comfort to know Hakim had died a hero.

Maggie hit play on the video.

"My name is Hakim Hasan. I'm eighteen years old and from Birmingham. I love my mum, like wasting hours playing video games, and support Birmingham F.C., even though we're shit and never win anything."

Maggie laughed at that and wrapped her free arm around Ashton's.

"A few years ago, a terrorist group targeted my brother, Khalid. They manipulated him. Warped his brain into believing their lies. Looking back on it, I think Khalid was feeling lost. He had a bright future ahead of him and was the first person in our family to go to uni. Me and my mum were so proud of him."

Hakim coughed, and Maggie's hand came into view on the screen as she wiped the blood from his lips.

"Khalid killed ten people, and himself, in a suicide bombing. They say he yelled 'Allahu Akbar' before he did it. Some of you watching won't know what that means, but you've probably heard it on the news and stuff. It's a term we Muslims use to remind ourselves every day that God is greater than the ugliness of the world. Terrorists like Dabir Omar and the Acolytes are part of that ugliness. They're so filled with hate and use God's name in vain to carry out horrible acts."

Maggie sniffed, seeing the pain in Hakim's face as he struggled on, knowing he was about to die. Even in his last moments, Hakim had wanted to try and help. To make a change.

"I want to make it clear to you all, that they don't speak for us. Islam is a peaceful and beautiful faith, and everything they do goes against our beliefs. I know you're afraid. We are, too. But please don't lump us in with them in your mind. We're just like you."

Hakim was crying now, but he continued on, Maggie recalling how cold he was laying there on the hard floor.

"I'll never see it, but I hope that one day everyone will come together instead of breaking further apart. It's the only way to stop this mess from happening over and over again."

Hakim was visibly shaking now, his lips growing a cold shade as his body tremored.

"And to those out there who are doing what the Acolytes did to my brother; You will not win. Fear will not prevail. One day the world will unite as one, and on that day, you will fall."

The video stopped, and Maggie handed the phone back to Ashton. So far, Hakim's final words had been viewed over three million times. Maggie didn't know if it would make a difference if things really would change for the better, but like Hakim, she had hope.

And as long as she had hope, she could continue to fight against those who want to see the world burn.

"Come on," she said, turning from the graveyard below as the funeral ended. "I could use a drink."

"Now there's a plan," Ashton said, brightening up. "You buying?"

Maggie grinned and shook her head. "I was going to, but then I remembered you have that big expensive apartment in Paris."

Ashton laughed. "Touché."

Maggie didn't know what her future would hold. So much had changed over the last few months. Life altering things that made her a different person to the woman she was before. Things were far from perfect, but time would pass and help heal some of the wounds she'd collected.

And until then, she had her dear friend and some good whiskey to keep her company.

Thank you for reading THE DEFECTOR! If you enjoyed the book, I would greatly appreciate it if you could consider adding a review on your bookstore of choice.

Reviews make a huge difference to the success or failure of a book, especially for newer writers like myself. The more reviews a book has, the more people are likely to take a shot on picking it up. The review need only be a line or two, and it really would make the world of difference for me if you could spare the three minutes it takes to leave one.

With all my thanks,

Jack McSporran

fought beside. With no one to turn to, Maggie relies on the one person who has always had her back—herself.

From the hidden nightclubs of Madrid, to the dark streets of Moscow, Maggie must delve into the depths of the criminal underworld to unearth the truth, and fast. Because time is running out and the enemy is closer than she thinks...

<u>Get your copy of Kill Order today!</u>

CHAPTER I
CANNES, FRANCE
18 MAY

Maggie Black scanned the top deck of the luxury yacht and searched for her target.

A sea of people crowded the open space. Everyone from A-list actors and rock stars to wannabes and groupies were all there for the annual Cannes Film Festival. Even the patient onboard staff seemed impressed as they waited on Hollywood royalty.

The security guards were less impressed. Maggie made sure to keep an extra eye on them. They wandered among the guests in suits that strained against muscled arms, their postures rigid and wires barely hidden in their ears. Blending in wasn't on their list of priorities – unlike Maggie's.

"What did you say your name was again?" asked an irritating brunette to Maggie's left. The stench of cigarette smoke and vodka assaulted her with the woman's every breath.

"Eva," Maggie replied, swirling her glass of water on the rocks. She leaned against the rails of the balcony and looked over the woman's shoulder, feigning interest in whatever it was she was saying.

Music blared from a deejay booth in the center of the partial deck as people well past drunk danced under the glow of the moon, its light glittering off the water as the yacht bobbed a half mile out from the port.

"And what do you do?" the brunette asked, who'd introduced herself as Brooke. Or Becky. Or something like that.

"I'm a model." Maggie didn't bother looking at her conversation partner. She was far more interested in the guard nearest her, and the flash of his pistol as he adjusted his jacket. A black Smith and Wesson from the looks of it. Her hand itched for her own 9mm Glock 19, but it was back in her hotel room.

The crew had searched everyone before coming onboard, and her tight-fitting red dress could hardly conceal a weapon like that. Tonight, Maggie was armed with her wit and her fists.

"Funny, I don't recognize you," Brooke said, the hint of a sneer edging at the corner of her ruby lips.

"Most of my work is international. I did a shoot in Japan last week."

The shoot – two bullets in a Japanese businessman. One in his chest and one in the head to make sure. The British government didn't take too kindly to those caught selling malware to their enemies. In this case, a militia group planning a cyber-attack against the National Health Service.

Maggie flipped her waves of long blond hair to the side and turned to gaze over the deck below.

Plush sofas sat in clusters around glass tables, each of them covered with champagne bottles and bowls of suspicious-looking white powder piled high in the center.

She moved from face to face, evaluating then discarding them one by one. None of them matched the image of the reporter she'd memorized.

Then she saw him. Adam Richmond. Investigative reporter, trust fund playboy, and seller of classified information.

Brooke yapped in Maggie's ear about some movie producer she was seeing, but Maggie paid her no mind. She focused all her attention on the tall, dark, handsome man chatting up a beautiful woman near the bar.

The woman touched his arm and laughed at whatever Adam said. Her clear interest seemed to bore Adam, and his gaze moved from the woman to the rest of the party.

Condensation dripped down Maggie's glass as she took a sip. The day's heat lingered into the night, making Maggie's pale skin glow amid the humid air. The sky had bled out and bruised to a dark purple, promising another ideal day for the film festival. Though not everyone onboard would see the sun rise.

Adam's eyes traveled towards the top deck and landed on Maggie. He grinned at her, the woman beside him forgotten. Maggie watched him with open interest and tucked a strand of hair behind her ear.

He gestured to the bar, where a barman placed two glasses of bubbling champagne on the counter. *Smooth.*

Maggie abandoned her spot at the railing, leaving a flustered Brooke behind without a goodbye, and made her way to him. She took her time travelling down the stairs, allowing her leg to peek out from the slit of her dress, feeling his eyes take her in from head to toe.

As she reached the bottom step, Adam dug into his jacket pocket and brought a cellphone to his ear. His face grew serious as he spoke, his attention stolen from her. Maggie frowned. She made for the bar, but a group of partiers interrupted her path and blocked her view of the target.

When they dispersed, Adam was gone.

Maggie picked up her pace and reached the bar. "The man who was just standing here, where did he go?"

The barman shrugged, busy shaking cocktails and hounded with calls for service from the other guests.

Maggie scanned the bar, but Adam was nowhere to be found. *Shit.*

She scoured the whole deck in search for him, heat rising to her cheeks. A drunk man stumbled into her and stood on the bottom of her dress, pinning her to the spot. Maggie yanked the dress back and shoved the guy away from her. If only she could have worn trousers instead of an insufferable dress.

Holding the train away from her feet, she weaved through the party and headed inside, closing the heavy watertight door behind her.

The bass from the speakers outside hummed through the wooden floors, adding to the rocking of the water as Maggie hurried down the corridor. Her sea legs had suffered much worse than the tame waves of the Mediterranean, allowing her to move with ease, even in killer heels.

Passing a lounge area with a grand piano nestled in the corner, she smiled at those standing around it, singing songs and taking shots of amber liquid. *At least someone gets to enjoy the cruise,* she thought as she continued deeper into the heart of the yacht.

Maggie rounded a corner and took a flight of stairs leading down to the sleeping quarters on the deck below. Voices made her freeze.

"No," said a muffled voice. "I don't want to."

"Yes, you do." The second voice was deep. Slurred. "You've been hanging over me all night."

"Please."

"Shh," the male voice cooed. "You know you want it."

Maggie leaned down to get a look.

A man in his fifties had a young girl pinned against the wall, a meaty hand covering her mouth to stop her from calling out or screaming.

Maggie's nails dug into her palm. She continued down

the stairs and marched up behind the man. "Hey," she called, grabbing the man's shoulder.

"We're busy here." His scowl was soon replaced with a sloppy smile. He whistled, looking Maggie up and down. "Want to join in?"

Maggie grimaced at the man, whose shirt was soaked through with sweat. "Get your hands off her."

The man laughed and returned his focus to the frightened girl. "If you're not interested, piss off before I lose my patience."

Maggie took a deep breath. She couldn't afford to cause a scene or waste time. She needed to find Adam.

The man laughed at her and shook his head. "Stupid bitch."

Maggie grabbed him again and spun him around to face her. She smashed her fist into his bulbous nose, the bone cracking with a delicious snapping sound.

Blood flooded from his nostrils and ran down his chin.

"You broke my fucking nose!" The man lunged at her, but Maggie was ready for him. She caught him with a mean right hook, sending him crashing to the floor with a thump.

The girl leaned against the wall and blinked at Maggie. Her eyes were dilated, and black hair stuck to the sides of her face.

"You okay?" Maggie asked.

The girl stared at her knocked-out attacker and gave a little nod.

"Good. Get out of here and don't tell anyone what happened."

"What about him?" she asked.

"I'll deal with it. Now go, and make sure you drink plenty of water until the yacht gets back to the port." Cocaine and alcohol was one cocktail the girl could do without.

"I will. Thanks." The girl backed away then ran upstairs and out of sight.

Maggie rested her hands on her hips and sighed. She kicked the big lump with the tip of her shoe, then hoisted him up by the arms and dragged him into a nearby supply closet. Maggie shut the door and allowed herself a brief moment to catch her breath before moving on. The dead weight of the man, combined with the heat, sent trickles of sweat down her back.

The lower deck was deserted, the hum of the party echoing from above. Maggie walked towards the aft until the music died enough to hear waves sloshing against the sides of the yacht. She reached a wide hallway with numbered rooms running along either side. Someone had left a door ajar, which revealed a large suite with a king-sized bed and a private balcony.

Her reports said Adam Richmond was staying onboard the yacht during his stay in Cannes. One of his many high roller friends owned the vessel, an investment banker on Wall Street. Adam must have a private room. Somewhere.

Maggie strained her ears and listened for any signs of

life. She tried the first door, but it was locked. As was the next.

This is taking too long. Maggie felt around for the light switch. She flicked off the lights and allowed her eyes to settle. There. At the end of the row to the left.

Light emanated in a thin strip from under the bedroom door. She grinned. *Bingo.*

Maggie turned the lights back on and crept toward the door. She pressed her ear against the wood, careful to stay out of view from the peephole. Footsteps. She was sure of it.

Maggie gripped the door handle, hoping it wasn't locked, and turned it. The door swung open and she stumbled inside, pretending to lose her balance.

Adam jumped in his chair, closing his laptop before turning to face her.

"Oh," Maggie said, wobbling on her feet, "this isn't Brooke's room."

"No, it's not." Adam got up from his chair and ushered her towards the door. He stopped when he got up close to her, his face brightening. "You're the woman from the top deck."

"And you're the man from the bar." Maggie let out a laugh. "I'm sorry. I was looking for my friend, and I got the room numbers mixed up."

"A happy coincidence." Adam crossed the room and opened a minibar, taking out a bottle of cognac. "How about that drink?"

Maggie looked back out into the hall. "I should really be getting back."

"Oh, come on. Just one drink. I insist." Adam shot her a wide smile, his schoolboy charm laid on as thick as his upper-class drawl.

Maggie pretended to consider his offer and shrugged. "Well, if you *do* insist." She closed the door behind her with a soft *click*.

She eyed the closed laptop as Adam poured the drinks into curved crystal glasses. Maggie didn't know what secrets lay inside the hard drive or who the reporter planned on selling them to, but she knew one thing. The transaction would never take place. Not on her watch.

Adam returned and handed her a filled glass. He held his own to hers and they clinked their glasses.

"I'm Adam, by the way."

"Eva," Maggie said, biting her lip. She tossed back her glass in one gulp, and the cognac burned down her throat in a comforting warmth.

Adam's eyebrows rose and then he followed suit, smacking his lips.

"The party couldn't hold your attention?" Maggie asked, brushing her hand against his.

"Let's just say things have certainly picked up, thanks to you."

Maggie gave him a playful push. "Charmer."

He grinned at that, and Maggie suppressed the urge to roll her eyes. A light breeze swept in from the balcony, the curtain sweeping up like a phantom warning of things to come.

"I don't mean to be forward," he said, stepping closer so his chest pressed against hers, "but what would happen if I tried to kiss you right now?"

Maggie raised her head and whispered into his ear. "Why don't you try and find out?"

Adam closed his eyes and moved his head towards her with parted lips.

Maggie placed her hands at either side of his face and leaned towards him. Before Adam Richmond's lips could touch her own, she tightened her grip and jerked her hands with a savage twist.

His neck snapped. A clean, precise break.

They always were.

Maggie let go, and Adam collapsed to the floor, his head lolling to the side.

She stepped over him and sat down at the desk, the seat still warm from the reporter's body, which now grew cold on the floor.

She opened the laptop, took out a portable USB stick from her bra, and plugged it into the port at the side.

Taking a quick glance at the folders stored in the hard drive, Maggie transferred the files onto the USB.

Five percent complete. The green bar grew longer as each file downloaded. *Ten percent.*

A loud knock rapped on the door. "Mr. Richmond, are you okay? We heard a crash."

Maggie's heart leapt in her ribcage. The man's phrasing was not lost on her.

We.

Maggie tapped the side of the laptop. "Come on, come on."

Twenty percent complete.

Sliding out of her heels, Maggie slipped off her dress and stripped down to the thermal bathing suit concealed beneath. She leaned down and collected one of her heels.

Fifty percent complete.

Maggie stared at the body. The man behind the door called again. "Mr. Richmond? I'm coming in."

Bollocks.

The door swung open as Maggie charged across the room. She surprised the first guard, swinging her shoe to meet his head. The heel hit his temple, and blood spurted out like oil from a well.

The next guard was ready for her.

She sent a punch to Maggie's gut, forcing the air out her lungs. The woman reached for her gun, but Maggie charged into her side and rammed her against the door. Their impact slammed the door shut and they tripped over the fallen guard, who squirmed around like a fish out of water, holding his head to keep his brain inside.

Maggie scrambled to her feet, but the woman grabbed her hair and sent her reeling back.

She went with the momentum, hissing as hair ripped

out from her scalp. Maggie rolled into the fall and kicked up, her bare heel connecting with the woman's jaw.

The guard collapsed beside her now unconscious partner.

Maggie returned to the laptop, picking up the woman's gun as she went.

Eighty percent complete.

Footsteps sounded outside, coming closer. She counted four different gaits before she sent six rounds through the door.

Ninety-five percent complete.

There was a commotion outside the door, and it barged open, hitting the fallen guards.

Ninety-eight percent complete.

Someone grunted on the other side of the door as they shoved, sliding the fallen guards forward across the floor.

One-hundred percent complete.

Maggie pulled out the USB and scooped up the laptop. Behind her, the guards shoved the door open enough to fit through.

She reached the balcony and launched the laptop overboard. It landed in the water with a satisfying splash and sank to the murky depths below.

A call came from behind her as the first guard slipped through the gap. Maggie aimed and shot the guard through the thigh. He fell to the ground as three more entered the room and more guards shouted in the corridor.

Maggie dropped the gun and turned back to the

balcony. She ran forward and leapt in the air. Her body passed over the railings, and she positioned herself into a dive and met the water as gunshots carried out through the night.

CHAPTER 2
————
LONDON, GREAT BRITAIN
19 MAY

Maggie turned the keys in the lock and entered her apartment. A pile of letters lay on the floor waiting for her. She bent down with a groan, her muscles aching from the events of the night before, and nudged the door shut with her foot.

Bills, junk mail, bank statements, take out menus. Nothing important. She tossed them onto the kitchen counter with her keys, kicked off her boots, and wheeled her suitcase into her bedroom. She'd unpack later.

The air in the apartment was stale from disuse. Maggie lit a lemon scented candle, sitting it on the table beside the large living room windows. She peered out at the city skyline, the River Thames flowing past The O2 arena, illuminated like the towers behind it, which belonged to Canary Wharf's most influential banks.

Her reflection stared back at her. She looked tired, her

hair pulled back from her face and bags resting under her ice blue eyes.

Maggie turned away, taking off her coat and draping it over her leather corner couch. A red flickering light caught her attention, the answering machine blinking to alert her of a new message.

Just one. She hadn't been home for over two weeks.

Maggie played the message and plodded over to the fridge to appease her grumbling stomach. Empty, aside from a jar of pickles and a container of something that had long since passed its sell by date. Maggie dumped the container in the bin and ran a hand over her head.

The message played and a woman's voice filled the open plan living space.

"Hi, this is Laura from First Class Travel. I'm calling to fill you in on some of our latest deals as you bought a holiday from us eighteen months ago. I guess you're at work right now, so phone me back when you can. Remember, life isn't all work and no play. You deserve some down time, and we have the perfect hot spots for you to choose from. Bye for now."

Maggie deleted the message and stared at the now empty answering machine. It felt like all she did was travel, though never for pleasure. Even the trip Laura the travel agent mentioned went unused; Maggie was stuck undercover in Morocco at the time.

A familiar shadow crossed the floor of her balcony and pressed up to the sliding door.

Maggie let the black cat in, her only visitor to the river-side apartment since she bought the place last year.

"Hello, Willow." Maggie scratched the cat behind the ears.

Willow rubbed herself against Maggie and circled around her legs, purring up at her. For a stray, Willow was a rather affectionate feline.

Maggie rummaged through the cupboards in the kitchen in search of a can of tuna to feed her furry friend, but like the fridge, they were a barren wasteland.

Willow meowed.

"Chinese food it is then."

Maggie called the restaurant around the corner and placed her usual order. Thirty minutes later, her chicken chow mein and spring rolls arrived, along with steamed fish for Willow.

She switched on the TV, but nothing held her attention for long. There was a spy film showing on one of the movie channels, and Maggie laughed at the ridiculous gadgets featured. Give her an old-fashioned gun or knife any day.

Turning off the TV, Maggie finished her meal in peaceful silence. She fell back on her couch, still smelling as new as the day it arrived, and pulled her bare feet up, closing her eyes as Willow snuggled into her.

A few minutes later, Maggie was back on her feet, pacing around her unused home. It was always like that after a mission, especially one that involved wet work.

Unlike her television, Maggie couldn't simply press an off switch. She'd lost count of how many lives she'd taken over the years, her first at the ripe young age of fifteen. Perhaps she didn't want to know the number.

She could ring Ashton, but he would be busy. The man had never seen a Friday night he didn't like; not that he needed the weekend as an excuse to get up to no good. Besides, she hadn't spoken to him for almost a month. Hopping from one job to the next was a sure-fire way to annihilate any resemblance of a social life.

Her thoughts travelled to Leon, but Maggie was fast to shove them aside.

Fed and watered with a belly full of fish, Willow gave herself a shake, leapt off the couch, and left the way she came in, back out into the night and leaving Maggie alone.

It took all of five minutes before Maggie collected her computer from the coffee table and fired it up. She inserted the USB stick from her mission and downloaded the files she copied off Adam Richmond's computer.

Hours passed as Maggie combed over the contents, reading articles the reporter had penned himself, scrolling through emails from his work and personal accounts, and clicking from one image to the next in his photo folder.

It was almost midnight when she came across something that caught her eye, though it wasn't what she had expected to discover.

Maggie grabbed her mobile and rang one of the few

numbers stored in her contacts. The person at the other end answered after three rings.

"We need to meet."

CHAPTER 3

20 MAY

Maggie arrived at Westminster Station by way of Canning Town, maneuvering through the crowds of eager tourists and early risers, and up the stone steps out onto Bridge Street.

Big Ben watched her as she buttoned her jacket and crossed Parliament Street, continuing down Great George Street. A mass of enraged gray clouds hung over her, threatening rain in typical British fashion for the approaching summer.

She stopped into a café for a much-needed coffee and then cut through St. James's Park. Maggie stopped by the bridge and sipped her drink while she watched some children feed the ducks. Boisterous pigeons swooped down and stole the pieces of bread from their little hands with the skill of London's best thieves.

Maggie arrived at her destination soon after, staring up at the five-story office building on King Street that served as the Unit's headquarters. Disguised as Inked

International, a global stationery supplier, the boring nature of the business gave those not in-the-know no reason to walk through the doors.

The only time anyone ever tried to enter was when they stumbled home from The Golden Lion, an old-school pub next door where Maggie spent one too many nights drinking her way through their collection of whiskies in her early years as an agent.

Maggie swiped her security pass at the entrance. The locks clicked open, and Maggie walked to the elevators, her heels clacking on the marble floor. She entered the empty cab, pressed the button for the top floor, and waited.

"Hold on," came a voice before a foot wedged between the closing doors. The man pried them open and stood beside her in the confined space.

Maggie focused on keeping her face expressionless, her heart fluttering at the sight of him. She cleared her throat, the familiar woody scent of his favorite aftershave dancing in her nose.

"Hi, Leon."

"How you doing, Maggie?" he asked in his deep, gravelly voice.

"Just back from an assignment last night. You?"

"Can't complain." Leon hit the button for the fourth floor. "I thought you just came back from Japan the other week?"

"Are you keeping tabs on me?" Maggie craned her

neck to meet his dark brown eyes for the first time. At six foot three, Leon Frost had over half a foot on her.

"I worry, that's all," he said, his white shirt crisp and bright against his black skin. "Every agent needs some downtime after being out there."

"I'm a big girl, I can look after myself."

Leon sighed and rubbed a strong hand over his close-trimmed beard. "I didn't mean it like that."

It was always like that these days. Both with so much to say to each other, yet saying nothing at all.

They stood in awkward silence until the elevator pinged and opened at Leon's floor. He stepped out, and the cab felt empty without him.

Leon stopped and turned back to her. "You look good, Maggie."

"You too," she said, gripping onto her jacket sleeve.

The doors closed between them, and Maggie took a deep, shaking breath. Seeing Leon was never easy, especially when she wasn't prepared for it.

Straightening her back, she swept her feelings to the side as the elevator stopped on her floor. By the time she stepped out, she was back to normal, her training kicking in.

Never let anyone see you sweat.

Brice Bishop was waiting for her in his office with a cup of tea in his hand.

"Maggie," he said, the remnants of a Manchester accent still in his inflection. "Nice to have you back."

Maggie sat down across from his desk. "Thanks."

Bishop's office was clean and Spartan, the result of a long career in the military before he joined the Unit. His phone buzzed and he read the message, tossing it back on the desk with a heavy sigh.

"Everything okay?"

"June," said Bishop, needing no further clarification. The divorce with his wife had been a long and messy one, their relationship barely civil and only so because of their kids.

"What now?"

"I finally get the girls next weekend, and she's trying to cancel."

"Why?"

"She and *Brian*," he said, the distain for his ex-wife's new fiancé clear from the way he growled the man's name, "decided to take a family holiday that week. If I cancel, I don't get to see them for at least another three weeks."

"And if you don't, you're the bad one for cancelling their holiday," Maggie finished. It had taken a while for Bishop to get back on good terms with his teenage daughters, both girls siding with their mother during the divorce.

Bishop leaned back in his chair. "June's design, of course. She should have been an agent."

"I'm sorry, Bishop."

Bishop tried to shrug like it was nothing, but he didn't quite pull it off.

For a man in his late fifties, he still clung to his brown

hair which he kept cropped at the sides like he was still a soldier. Crow's feet perched at the corners of his eyes, his skin tough as leather, and nose bent out of shape from when Maggie had broken it during her first official mission.

To the untrained eye, Bishop appeared as just another businessman living in London who looked after himself and wore expensive suits. It was all deliberate, of course. Brice Bishop was so much more than that, and stories of his days as an agent still passed around the Unit like folktales. He was one of the best.

"Enough about that. I trust everything went well?"

Maggie nodded. "All according to plan."

"Excellent."

"There was one thing."

"Oh?"

"I couldn't find any of the stolen secrets on Richmond's laptop." Not one file. She searched for hidden folders and encrypted documents disguised as something else, but the laptop was empty.

"You read the computer files?"

"I figured I should check what the secrets were, in case any of them were an imminent threat to national security." And out of sheer curiosity to find out what was so classified that Richmond had to die, but Maggie kept that to herself.

Bishop nodded. "Good thinking."

Maggie leaned forward in her chair. "But that's just it. I didn't find any."

"Nothing?" Bishop frowned.

"Not nothing, but not what we were looking for."

Maggie got up and turned on the computer. It was linked to a projector Bishop used when hosting meetings. Like she did at her apartment, she plugged in the USB stick and selected some of the files of note.

"I trolled through every file on here. Junk for the most part, but one folder in particular stood out." Maggie clicked the first file and it appeared on the projector screen on the wall. "Richmond was working on a story, investigating a private and commercial property developer named Brightside Property and Construction Limited."

Bishop clasped his hands. "What was his angle?"

"Corruption. Apparently, the company applied for planning permission on a plot of land in the East End, but it was declined." Richmond had acquired a copy of the application to prove it.

"Why?"

Maggie brought up an article that had made it onto the BBC News website. "The land is home to a row of government assisted houses owned by the local council. The residents are refusing to move."

"Where does the corruption come in?" Bishop asked, his tea growing cold on the desk.

"Brightside recently purchased the houses from the government, which now makes the homes private rentals.

Brightside increased the rent payments to unaffordable levels to push the residents out."

Bishop shook his head. "Legally evicting them. Sly bastards."

"It's worked for the most part," Maggie continued, "but a few of the residents are causing a stink about it and going to the press. There have been reports of intimidation, too. Residents claim men knocked on their doors in the middle of the night and threatened them, warning them to move."

Richmond had gathered some written testimonies and a few names, but nothing concrete. It didn't take long for Maggie to find a way into the Metropolitan Police's records and hunt down police reports to corroborate the stories.

"I did some digging. Similar reports have been made against Brightside in other developments in London and surrounding areas over the years."

Maggie clicked on another file. A photo of a body appeared on the screen, an old man beaten to death, his face purple and swollen.

"Eric Solomon was found dead in his home, the victim of a supposed break-in."

Bishop examined the photos on the screen. "What makes you think he wasn't?"

"The week before his body was found, Mr. Solomon turned down a substantial financial offer from Brightside to move. He'd purchased the council house he was living in before Brightside took over and procured the surrounding land. His refusal to move would have stopped their plans to knock down the houses and build a shopping center on the land."

Maggie brought up the proposed plans for the construction. Richmond had really done his homework.

"With the old man dead, Brightside could carry on with their plans," Bishop said, tying up all the pieces with a neat bow.

"That's what I'm thinking." Maggie pulled the USB from the computer. "Though it seems strange for someone like Adam Richmond to investigate all this while preparing to sell classified documents to the highest bidder."

"Perhaps it was part of his cover," ventured Bishop. "He was an investigative reporter after all."

Bishop could be right. Maggie sat back down and slid the USB across the desk to him. "I don't know all the big players yet, but I will soon enough. I'm pretty sure Richmond was on to something here. Something big."

"Great work. Really." Bishop leaned back in his chair. "I'll speak with the Director General and see if she can dig anything up from the guys at MI5. They might already be looking into the dealings of this company." He shook his head. "Richmond must have kept the stolen files somewhere else."

"I can contact Ms. Helmsley if you want," Maggie offered. The Director General was known as a pit bull in a power suit around the Unit, but Maggie liked her. She had a knack for seeing through bullshit and kept the men running around for her like they were little boys and she their headmistress.

"No, that's all right, I'll do it." Bishop slid a manila folder in front of her. "I have a favor to ask of you in the meantime."

"What?" Maggie eyed the folder but didn't pick it up.

"The Mayor of London is the keynote speaker at an international business conference in the financial district and has requested a chaperone."

Maggie sighed. "When?"

"Tonight," said Bishop. "Nina will be there, too, following the same orders for the Foreign Secretary."

"Why can't another agent do it?" The last thing Maggie wanted to do was go back out on a mission. She'd only just gotten home. "I saw Leon coming in."

"Leon is already assigned to another case. All my other agents are tied up."

Maggie remained quiet. If she wanted a career in babysitting, she would've been a nursery teacher.

"It's only for a couple of hours," added Bishop, giving her that pleading look she hated.

Maggie drooped her shoulders. "I can look after them both on my own. No need to send two agents for this type of job." If she wasn't getting the night off, at least Nina could.

"Nina is going, too. You really need to learn to work

with others," Bishop said, not for the first time. "You can't do everything on your own."

Maggie folded her arms. It wasn't that she didn't like Nina. They had known each other since they joined the Unit at sixteen. She just worked better alone. "Fine, but I'm taking my annual leave after this."

"Of course." Bishop handed her the file containing what she would need to know for the evening's event. "Thanks, Maggie."

Maggie took the manila folder and left Bishop's office. Maybe she would call that travel agent back after all.

CHAPTER 4

The taxi took a left from Leadenhall Street and turned into St Mary Axe, where a swanky new hotel had opened on the corner of Bevis Marks, right next to The Gherkin.

Maggie paid the fare and stepped out into the cold. The sky's earlier promise of rain came through, and huge droplets plummeted down from the heavens.

She ducked under the covered entrance to the Baltic Hotel and shook her umbrella out.

"I'll take that for you, Madam," said a man by the door, ushering her inside.

"Thank you," she said. "I'm here for the conference."

The man pointed across the room to where a sign stood for the event. "Straight ahead."

Maggie walked through the foyer and arrived at a large and glamorous conference room, decked out with chandeliers hanging from the high ceilings that overlooked round tables. At the back of the conference room, Maggie noted the podium where the mayor would give his talk.

The tables were set with fine porcelain dishes, crystal glassware, and golden cutlery. The staff had even arranged the napkins into elegant swans. Ten seats a piece were tucked under the tables, upholstered in fine gold suede to match the intricate filigree design of the wallpaper.

Along the bar sat buckets of champagne resting on ice, ready for when the attendees arrived.

The organizers had spared no expense, appropriate given the high-profile guests could bring millions of pounds in foreign investments into London's private sector.

Nina stood waiting for her near the bar as staff milled around the room making final touches to the pristine layout.

"I've scoped out the place," announced Nina by way of hello. "Everything's in order."

She wore a sleek gown with a plunging neckline, the emerald fabric bringing out the green in her hazel eyes. It also did a good job of hiding the knives Maggie knew would be strapped to Nina's thighs. She had a fondness for getting up close and personal with her enemies.

"Good," replied Maggie, taking a quick look around. "Where are our charges?"

"Upstairs in one of the suites," Nina said as she headed out to the foyer and climbed the stairs.

Maggie followed, cursing the dress code. Why did she always find herself stuck in a dress? At least the black number she wore tonight wasn't hugging her hips. Her gun sat in its holster around her thigh, the familiar weight like a deadly comfort blanket.

"Here's your ear piece." Nina handed it over to Maggie along with a clipboard, both playing the role of event coordinators for their cover.

"It's already wired in to the right frequency." Nina spoke into the little microphone of her own device. "Testing."

"One, two, three," Maggie replied, securing hers around her ear, careful not to disturb her chignon hairdo. If she had to wear a dress, the least her hair could do was to stay out of her face.

"How was Cannes?" Nina asked, slowing down to walk by Maggie's side.

They were around the same height, but where Maggie was curved with vulpine features, Nina was lithe and all sharp angles, from her cutting cheekbones to her pointed nose.

"A pain in the neck," Maggie said. "The weather was nice though."

Nina shook her head. "Bishop really needs to stop sending me to places that require thermals."

"That's what you get for speaking Russian."

Nina huffed, a playful grin edging her lips. "You speak it, too, and you got to party on a yacht."

Maggie held up her hands. "Hey, I'm not complaining."

"Must be nice being the favorite," Nina teased, nudging her.

While preferring to work alone, if Maggie had to work with anyone, she was glad it was Nina. They were both teenagers when Bishop recruited them. Though they viewed each other as rivals at first, it didn't take long for them to become good friends. There weren't many women in the Unit, so they bonded quickly.

Like most old boys' clubs, the Unit had some work to do to bridge the gender imbalance. One too many meetings suffered from an overload of alpha-male testosterone. Not that Maggie or Nina had any trouble being heard. They just had to trample on a few toes first.

When they reached the third floor, Nina led Maggie to the corner suite, walking past two armed men who stood sentry before the entrance. Nina stopped in front of the door. "Fair warning, the Foreign Secretary is rather sloshed."

"Some boys just can't handle their drink," Maggie said with a sigh.

Nina ran a hand through her locks of straight chestnut hair and gave Maggie a wink.

The suite was as expected, given how the rest of the Baltic Hotel was decorated. The designers were fans of gold and rich creams, the primary colors of the sitting area that separated the bedrooms and bathroom. White lilies bloomed in several vases around the space and filled the air with their light floral scent.

A man got up from the couch on unstable legs. Nina was right, George Moulton was drunk, and from the triple measure in his hand, he had no intentions of stopping.

"Very nice indeed," he said, his voice loud and irritating. He studied them with glassy eyes, his fake tan a shade too orange to fool anyone into thinking it was real. "Why does Bishop only recruit sexy girls?"

Maggie responded with a raised eyebrow, biting her tongue to refrain from assassinating him with a response. At least she wasn't in charge of babysitting him for the night.

Nina stiffed at the mention of Bishop. "Is anyone else here?" she hissed.

"Relax, it's just us," said Moulton, shaking his head.

Nina glared at him.

Knowledge of the Unit was strictly classified due its propensity to cross the line of what was legal. Only those with a high enough clearance were made aware of its existence. Most of those working for the Secret Intelligence Service weren't even privy to their clandestine faction.

Ignoring the Foreign Secretary, Maggie walked over to the other man in the room. The Mayor of London was busy reading over notecards by the window. "Nice to meet you Mr. Worthington," she said and offered her hand. "I'm Maggie Black."

"A pleasure, and please, call me James," he said, his shake nice and firm. "Thank you for doing this on such short notice. I'm afraid our little event resulted in some anonymous threats, and Brice felt some extra security was in order."

"He doesn't like to take any chances," replied Maggie, cursing Bishop. She could be curled up on her couch in her pajamas, reading a good book with a nice glass of wine right about now.

George Moulton cackled behind them, Nina giggling a polite yet strained laugh along with him. James scowled at the man's back and offered Maggie an apologetic shrug.

"Ready for your speech?" Maggie asked.

"As I'll ever be." James released a heavy exhale. "I'm not good with these things."

James Worthington was new in his role as mayor. His predecessor Edgar Johnston died at the beginning of the year.

The new mayor was a handsome man, in a stiff upper lip sort of way. Not a hair was out of place on his head, his face clean shaven. He wore a smart suit, yet nothing too flashy like the Armani suit Moulton had squeezed into.

Moulton continued spluttering behind them, cracking jokes and lighting a cigar. Maggie had heard better one liners from Christmas crackers. The tendrils of smoke from his cigar circled around the room, drowning out the fresh lilies.

Maggie lowered her voice. "I'm sure you'll do better than him."

That won her a smile. "Yes, well, there's that at least."

"I'm going to take Mr. Moulton down to his table," called Nina. Moulton wasn't due to talk until after the dinner. Hopefully by then he would have the ability to stand, never mind give a speech on UK business.

"See you down there." Maggie turned back to the mayor when the door closed behind Nina. "We've made a sweep of the hotel and surrounding areas and cleared the conference room itself. You're good to go."

"Excellent." James held out his arm. "Shall we?"

Maggie indulged him and linked her arm in his. "It's a nice hotel," she said as they walked downstairs, the armed men following close behind. Voices travelled up from the foyer as the guests arrived in time for the mayor's speech. And the free booze and food.

"Yes, named after the Baltic Exchange. Terrible business."

Maggie was too young to remember the bombing of the building, right on the very street they were in now, but

Bishop had worked on the case. Three people had died that day, and another ninety-one injured.

"The drunken idiot is seated and behaving himself," came Nina's voice in Maggie's ear. "No signs of trouble."

The podium was to the back of the conference room and had its own entrance. The mayor stood behind the curtain, going over his notes one last time before going out.

The real event coordinator was behind the podium, too, ordering helpers around, her cheeks flush and movements flustered.

Maggie watched everyone who came and went, taking in faces and checking all access points.

"All clear here," Maggie said into her microphone just as a man caught her eye.

He strode backstage, but not in an organized rush like the others around him. He moved with a purpose, and that purpose became clear as he approached and reached into his jacket.

Maggie was about to shout when the man lunged at the mayor.

The man pulled out his gun and aimed at his target. Maggie dived in front of the mayor, blocking the man's path. His finger inched toward the trigger, but Maggie got to him first, thrusting his arm into the air. The gun went off and shot into the ceiling, flecks of plaster falling around them like snow.

Screams erupted from the other side of the curtain as guests heard the shot echoing off the walls of the large room. Chairs scraped on the floor and footsteps stampeded as people spilled out of the conference room and into the foyer.

The man was fast, and before the mayor's two personal guards could move three paces, he shot bullets into each of their heads. They crumbled to the floor like lifeless dolls, blood already seeping out of the bullet holes.

Maggie jabbed at the assailant, but he blocked her punch, sending a ringing pain through her arm. He pointed his gun at the mayor once again, but Maggie timed a perfect roundhouse that sent the weapon flying from his grasp.

The gun landed out of sight and Maggie squared up to the assassin, making sure to stay between him and James. If he wanted to reach the mayor, he would need to go through her.

The assassin swung a fist at her, and Maggie ducked back avoiding impact. She reached for her own gun, concealed around her thigh, but the man was on her again, this time catching her in the jaw with a right hook.

Maggie's head snapped to the side, the metallic tang of blood filling her mouth.

With a yell, she bounded forward and kneed him in the stomach, doubling him over. When he straightened back up, he had a knife in his hand, the silver glinting under the light.

The mayor stepped toward her, but Maggie shoved him back out of the way.

The assassin took advantage of her distraction and sliced at her. Maggie noticed the knife at the last second and flinched back, the blade catching on the fabric of her dress. She grabbed his wrist and thrust her palm into the man's elbow, aiming for a break. The bone didn't snap, but the assassin yelped and dropped his weapon.

But the loss of his weapon didn't slow him down. The man spun and rammed into her with his shoulder, forcing Maggie back. He swept his foot across the floor and swiped his leg into hers, sending her careening to the floor in a graceless fall.

He made for the mayor, but Maggie scrambled to her feet and grabbed him by the back of his collar, using his momentum as he stumbled back to trip him up. He fell on the arm she damaged and hissed.

Maggie seized the moment and threw all her weight into a brutal kick to his abdomen. The man groaned a curse and rolled away, holding his stomach as he bounced back up on agile feet. Maggie made for him again, but he turned and ran, heading back the way he came.

"Stay here. Don't come out until I come back for you," she ordered the mayor. "Got it?"

James nodded, wide eyed and panting, leaning against the wall to keep him steady.

Certain he was okay and had heard her, Maggie abandoned her heels, leaped over the dead bodies of the guards, and sped off after the assassin.

The foyer was pandemonium, people pushing and shoving each other out of the way to race from the hotel, all pretense of civility gone. An old man lay on the floor covering his head as others trampled over him to get to safety.

Nina spoke in Maggie's ear. "Maggie what the hell is going on? I heard gun shots."

"Someone tried to take out the mayor," she replied. "I'm in pursuit."

"Where are you? Do you need my help?"

"No. Get the Foreign Secretary out of here. He could be a target, too."

"Copy that," Nina said, her voice cutting in and out. "Go catch the prick."

The alarm interfered with the wire's signal, and it screeched in Maggie's ear. She took it out and tossed it, continuing her chase.

Maggie fought her way through the crowd, eyes set on finding the one responsible for the chaos. Black hair, light brown skin, an unassuming face that blended in well. Spanish from the way he cursed, though she could be mistaken on that. Spanish wasn't on her list of fluent languages.

The alarms wailed through the hotel. New and louder

screams followed, the sirens only panicking the people more.

Event Security tried to settle everyone down and restore order, but it wasn't working. The flight instinct in the guests was well and truly in effect. But not for Maggie. She was in full fight mode.

Maggie spotted Nina across the foyer in a splash of emerald among the crowd, heading out the front door with George Moulton. They met each other's eyes, and Maggie nodded for her to go on. George could be in danger.

Maneuvering her way through the panicked people, Maggie scanned every inch of the room.

There.

The assassin had made it through the crowd and was running up the stairs Maggie had taken with the mayor. The man looked over his shoulder and spotted her moving his way.

Maggie ran, feet cold on the marble floor, and fought her way through the guests. She reached the stairs and took them three at a time, releasing her gun from its holster and gripping it with a firm hold.

She turned the safety off and made it to the second floor.

A door to her left was closing, but no one had come racing out to head downstairs. Maggie caught it before it clicked shut and ducked inside, weapon at the ready.

The tail of a black jacket flashed down the hall as someone turned the corner at a run.

Maggie sprinted after them, her heart pounding and hair slipping out from behind her head. She rounded the corner and laid eyes on her target. Aiming with both hands, Maggie kept running and shot at the assassin.

The bullets missed his head by inches, embedding into the wall. He made a right down another hall of the hotel floor, and Maggie heard a crash.

Sprinting after him, she spotted the busted door to one of the rooms, the wood split off the frame. Gun at the ready, Maggie stepped inside. Something cold brushed against her bare foot, and she stole a glance down. A card. She bent to collect it, keeping her weapon pointed into the darkness of the room. It was a room key, but not for that one, or any other on the second floor. It was for the level above.

"I know you're in here," Maggie said, stepping inside.

Glass shattered further in, and she stormed through, ready to attack.

The assassin was at the window, the cold air blowing in through the broken pane. He took one last look at her before Maggie pulled the trigger.

The man jumped from the window and fell out of sight.

Maggie moved to the window and looked down. He wasn't there.

"Shit."

Things were still up in the air when she returned to the foyer, red faced and kicking herself at failing to apprehend the assassin.

She went to the back of the podium to return to the mayor and report what happened. So much for an easy couple of hours.

Maggie walked in to find the place deserted other than the two bodies lying in a heap on the ground.

She froze.

Not two bodies. Three.

James Worthington, Mayor of London and her charge, was dead.

Get your copy of Kill Order today!